Fayrouz Khaled graduated from the Faculty of Languages, MSA University, Cairo and has been pursuing her passion for screenwriting in MetFilm School, London. Fayrouz grew up in a family of journalists and writers, which inspired her to develop her great passion for writing at a very young age.

The modern world hurts so much, doesn't it? People now mistake sensitivity, empathy, and vulnerability for weakness. This is for the ones who suffered pain, depression, and anxiety. This is for the ones who are struggling to find who they are in a world that demands them to be something else. You are not alone, I feel you, I know you, And I love you. To my brother, my second father, my best friend, and my greatest supporter. Thank you for always believing in me.

Fayrouz Khaled

LOST IN THE ECHO

AUSTIN MACAULEY PUBLISHERS™
LONDON • CAMBRIDGE • NEW YORK • SHARJAH

Copyright © Fayrouz Khaled (2021)

The right of Fayrouz Khaled to be identified as author of this work has been asserted by the author in accordance with Federal Law No. (7) Of UAE, Year 2002, Concerning Copyrights and Neighboring Rights.

All rights reserved. No part of this publication may be reproduced, stored in a retrieval system, or transmitted in any form or by any means; electronic, mechanical, photocopying, recording, or otherwise, without the prior permission of the publishers.

Any person who commits any unauthorized act in relation to this publication may be liable to legal prosecution and civil claims for damages.

The age category suitable for the books' contents has been classified and defined in accordance to the Age Classification System issued by the National Media Council.

ISBN – 9789948452249 – (Paperback)
ISBN – 9789948452232 – (E-Book)

Application Number: MC-10-01-4695176
Age Classification: 17+

Printer Name: iPrint Global Ltd
Printer Address: Witchford, England

First Published (2021)
AUSTIN MACAULEY PUBLISHERS FZE
Sharjah Publishing City
P.O. Box [519201]
Sharjah, UAE
www.austinmacauley.ae
+971 655 95 202

Table of Contents

Prologue	9
Chapter One 16 Years Old	12
Chapter Two 12 Years Old	18
Chapter Three 12 Years Old	20
Chapter Four 12 Years Old	23
Chapter Five 15 Years Old	26
Chapter Six 17 Years Old	30
Chapter Seven 20 Years Old	35
Chapter Eight Now 21 Years Old	39
Chapter Nine	43
Chapter Ten	47
Chapter Eleven	56
Chapter Twelve	60
Chapter Thirteen 18 Years Old	64
Chapter Fourteen Now	71
Chapter Fifteen	74
Chapter Sixteen	80
Chapter Seventeen	86
Chapter Eighteen	92
Chapter Nineteen	95

Chapter Twenty	98
Chapter Twenty-One	102
Chapter Twenty-Two	109
Chapter Twenty-Three	116
Chapter Twenty-Four	121
Chapter Twenty-Five	129
Chapter Twenty-Six	133
Chapter Twenty-Seven	139
Chapter Twenty-Eight	148
Chapter Twenty-Nine	156
Chapter Thirty	167
Chapter Thirty-One	176
Chapter Thirty-Two	182
Chapter Thirty-Three	190
Chapter Thirty-Four	197
Chapter Thirty-Five	206
Chapter Thirty-Six	218
Chapter Thirty-Seven	222
Chapter Thirty-Eight	225

Prologue

Why do you deny my existence?
Why do you insist on repressing everything that I am in you?
You realize I am there only when all your defense mechanisms have failed you, when anxiety hits you hard, and you have nothing left except me.
I have been here since the beginning of time. I am the senses, the feelings, and the meaning of life. No matter how hard you try, you cannot ignore me. You cannot deny me. You cannot erase me.
I am here to stay.
I know what you humans say about me, "Feelings can be ugly and unpleasant." But it's okay. I know I am not all about beauty, but I am always there to tell you something. Something that you usually choose to ignore.
Humans feel. Your whole existence is built upon feelings and even though sadly you do not communicate with me, you must know that I am always there.
I will consume you from the inside, until there is nothing left except for you to recognize me. There will be nothing left to hide. And when that happens, dear humans of the Earth, it's going to be destructive for you all. Do not ignore me. Just don't.
Do not talk about me to the wrong people.
And if you have no one to talk to, then write me down, paint me on canvas, sing me loud and clear, dance me till you're calm. Let it all out. Let out all of me that is left inside you. Face the unpleasant side of me. Face the scary side of me. Face that which has been killing you.
Befriend yourself, for once.

Feelings cannot be ignored. I can't be ignored. No matter how much you try.

I have noticed great changes in the human race lately. I notice how you try so hard to balance me against logic, my partner. It is a hard equation, I understand, but we are not here for war, we are here for you.

I am here for you.

I am here to help you notice the details.

I am here to help you smell the breeze instead of just breathing.

I am here to make you taste the water instead of just drinking.

I am here to make you notice the colors of the sky instead of just walking.

I am here to make you listen to music and hear the morning birds in the trees instead of that noise that surrounds you.

I am here to make you feel the silk, feel your lover's touch on your face, feel their embrace, and put your hand on their chest to feel their heartbeat.

I am here to let you know that you are not alone.

I am here to assure you that in the end I exist inside everyone.

However, everyone can experience the same thing, but feel it differently. That's the beauty I love most about my existence inside you all. No two people experience me the same way, ever. I have noticed you humans corrupting everything that I am. Nobody notices me or realizes how much I can affect you, and how much you humans misuse and misunderstand me. It's not that my partner logic has taken over, like you have always assumed. What really took over is materialism, hate, love of power, and selfishness.

You cannot kill me. But some of you have succeeded in giving up on me, in your desire to win things, gain positions and get stuff that is not valuable, or even half as precious as I am. You have left me behind and decided to notice me only in what consumes you to become the worst possible version of yourself.

Why did you misuse me so much?

I was only there to make you notice the unnoticeable. To make you realize that life is more than just the system you created; the system that soon ruined me and everything I stand for inside of you. You and your deathly, uncreative, unreliable, unhappy ways, systems, and rules. You and all your positions, power, wars, and illusions.

I did not come here to be misused and misunderstood.

I did not come here to be the motive for your horrible doings.

I came here to make you better. But you disappointed me. Some of you are still trying to survive in the globe of corrupted emotions.

So, I have decided to send a messenger of feelings; someone who will save humanity from what it has turned out to be. Someone who wasn't supposed to be born yet, but came to the world knowing nothing but me.

I gave her everything that I am.

She is the empath, the one who will save your world.

Chapter One
16 Years Old

A guy committed suicide yesterday, I remind myself while standing on the railing of our tenth-floor balcony. A human committed suicide, and everyone is carrying on with their lives, because why would they stop? If you know our country, you'll know that we have one of the lowest suicide rates. However, sometimes families do not like to share such incidents. Our religion, here in Egypt, views suicide as a sin. It makes sense at times, but then again how can a person suffering from depression or mental illness make any sense of anything?

"Should I jump?" I ask myself, still standing on the edge and inhaling the sweet June breeze of this Cairo morning. I am sun-soaked. Our penthouse overlooks the Nile; it is beautiful, and the weather is marvelous.

"It seems like a beautiful day to die!"

Death can be peaceful; to live in a much better place than the one we live in here on Earth. Death is peaceful; going to a divine place where there are no struggles, no pain, no loneliness, and no need to be anything that you are not. Death is peaceful in so many ways, so peaceful in fact that sometimes life seems meaningless. In the end, though, we all reach this peace. The peace of death. I smile and throw my head back, breathing in the breeze. The best thing about this country is that it's never really cold, or at least, that's what other people love about it. I, on the other hand, prefer the cold weather. I love its melancholy and its profound vibes that only I feel. The lost, empty emotions. Just like how I feel right now.

Empty, lost, angry, and absolutely insane, or at least, that's what people think.

I could do a back flip here, maybe, and land in the splits. Except I am not yet able to do this. I am practicing though—practice, practice, practice, practice. The only thing that has any meaning in my empty, irritating life.

I hear a voice shouting from behind me and know immediately that it is Fatma, the maid. I like her; the voices coming from her are all sincere, kind, and a bit broken at times. She is broken because she has too much work to do, and so little time. Or because her husband beats her up, just because he is a man and he can do what he likes. Poor minds.

The voice coming from Fatma now is not only the shouting; her emotions are loud too. She is scared, horrified even. I ignore her; I don't look because I know that if I do, she will only give me that look again. The look that questions my behavior, my ways, and my actions. Everyone looks at me like I am insane. It's not like I care, but it gets annoying. I feel a hand grabbing mine and I almost lose balance. Am I going to fall? Is this it? Am I going to die? My right foot almost hangs off the edge but then Fatma grabs me as hard as she can. I fall to the ground and Fatma is still holding my arm, only grabbing harder with her chubby hands and now it's starting to hurt a little.

"What are you doing, Malikah? Are you insane?" Fatma screams in my face and I know she means well. I know she is just scared. I know she is in a panic because she doesn't understand. She doesn't understand why someone born into a great famous family, with money and power, would be crazy enough to stand on the edge. Not caring if they die or live. She might also be starting to cry because she is sad from witnessing such a scene. Fatma is pretty sensitive; I hear her emotions. They are so loud.

"Insane, that's the word," I respond, smiling. "Maybe I *am* insane Fatma, let's believe that from now on, shall we?" I stand up and she lets go of my hand. I walk away, leave the roof terrace, and walk towards the living room. I know she is still sitting on the floor, stunned, she still feels all those emotions. She is scared and stunned because I'm acting like nothing has happened, as if standing on the edge is just another enjoyable sport. Even though there are no crash mats down there and falling will probably make me die. But yes, that's what I do. I am insane, remember?

This is not a suicide attempt, I remind myself, although I know that Fatma thinks otherwise. Suicide is loss of hope and I never had hope in the first place. So how could I lose it?

Am I insane? Or is it just my powers affecting me as usual? Sometimes, I don't know what's real and what's not; what emotions belong to me and what emotions belong to others. It's confusing.

The thing is that I hear voices.

Not just any voices.

I hear emotions. I hear the feelings that are buried deep down into the human soul, in the subconscious. The truth behind the lies, the disguised love, the anxiety, the stress, the manipulation, and the fears. If only humans would admit what they feel, if only humans would share the reality of their emotions, of their lives, of themselves. We might all get along as a human race if we truly communicate. But there goes technology, presenting a false image of perfection and how life is supposed to be, a false perspective, brainwashing our minds with social media. No one is what they seem, anymore.

I don't read minds, I just feel, and I think it's lame.

In fact, I feel more than any human can handle. These feelings, the voices I hear, the vibes I feel, they drive me crazy. I don't even know why I am the way I am, or if I am the only one. I don't talk about it and no one else knows anything about it, but god damn it, it drives me crazy. I hear everything; the lies, the manipulation, the love, the hate, the anger, the apathy, everything. I hear the feelings people desperately try to hide. Even the darkest ones, the ones that hunt at night.

It's hard to take it in, hard to handle, hard to realize. And because of this supernatural power, this empathy, I turn into an impulsive, angry person. I am trapped inside my head and no one can get me out. Some would say I am beyond help, and

I think I believe that too. I guess I am just another human hiding my emotions, trapped like everyone else. The difference is that I *know* I am trapped. I realize that the world around me wants nothing except to control me. Others do not realize it yet, or maybe they just deny it.

I stood on the railings today because I wanted to know what it would feel like. I can't stop thinking about the guy who committed suicide yesterday. He jumped 187 meters from the Cairo tower. That's higher than the pyramid itself. I think about that, and I think about all the reasons that could push a person to suicide. It's sad. No, it's not just sad, it is inexplicable.

I hate my powers, but if only I had known this guy, if only I had talked to him, and felt what he felt, then maybe I could have saved him. I hope someone feels me like I feel others. I wish I could have saved this guy even though I didn't know him. I too am a person suffering from anxiety and panic attacks. It's hard to fit in, I know.

No one knows anything about my power, or how much I suffer. My father denies there is a problem, because he is a middle-aged middle eastern man who unfortunately doesn't understand the importance of therapy. He thinks it's for crazy people. My father is a very knowledgeable man. He is very sophisticated, very elegant, very arrogant, very self-centered, and a great dictator. Yet despite all this, he still believes that therapy is not necessary. Some people still feel embarrassed or weird about therapy.

"Talk to me," he would say. As if I could ever talk to him.

Man, if you got inside my head you'd run away, screaming.

In a perfect world, humans would actually communicate. They would actually listen before they speak; they would actually sympathize and use empathy to feel one another. To actually help each other. In a perfect world, my mom would never have left me behind; my father would have felt my need to have him close, and my friends would have accepted me the way I am. In a perfect world, humans would have been kinder; jealousy and evil would never have existed in the dictionary. And love, love would be the center of the universe. Not money, not power, not fame, not this fake, virtual, and completely plastic world we live in.

But the world is not perfect, is it? And, if you think about it, perfection is such an overrated and impossible goal to chase. But what we live in is far from perfect, far from moderate, far from mediocre. What we live in now is chaos, anger, and lies. Maybe I am looking at the world through a broken lens, but surely someone, somewhere must feel the same way as me. And if there isn't anyone, well, it wouldn't be the first time I'd be the outcast.

I am the outcast in my own home.

If I were to give this age a name, I would call it "The Great Depression."

According to Existentialism, anxiety is what happens when we discover something that makes us doubt the things we know about our universe. According to my own understanding of the world, we are all born pure, and with no experience at all. Throughout our lives as humans we grow, acquire knowledge, learn from experiences, and create our own consciousness of how we view the world. Every person has an idea about how their life should go, and how it should be, and usually this is shaped by what society feeds us every day. Society is the brain washing mechanism that we grow up to believe in. We grow up to believe that marriage means stability, that wearing brands means you are unique, that fame means happiness, that people who haven't been to college are not educated, and that humans should follow a certain norm and tradition in everything.

Twelve years of school, four or more years in college, according to your major, then marriage, kids, and then death. I think the human race is beyond help.

What if this is not what I want to be? What if these are not the rules I want to follow? Who said that this simulated society is the only right? In this age, social media invades our minds. We believe everything we see, yes. But this doesn't prove what is true and what is not. But then, really, what is true? I hear it in the voices that no one else can hear. I hear the truth. But I guess societal brain washing is more convincing than a crazy girl with voices in her head.

We have so many means of communication, but we are still disconnected. We have all the freedom to choose to be something, but we all choose to be anything except who we really are. Even myself. I know I am not embracing who I am meant to be. If I did, people would call me insane. Oh, but they already call me that anyway.

We hide behind screens, behind pictures with filters. We hide behind the simulator we are put in from the day we are born. Nothing is really what it seems. Everyone is suffering one way or another—even those who believe in such false rules about how life should be lived. People look at someone and think that they are living an extraordinary life. But in fact, they are the most depressed. Societal norm isn't really what it should be, nothing should be anything.

No one should be anything. Norms, traditions, society's way of thinking is all an illusion that is created to feel like we belong. Like there are some kind of rules so we won't lose our way. But what about those people who do not belong? The people who do not feel like they fit in, no matter how much they try? The ones who realize everything I am saying, but have no idea what to do about it?

I do not want to live like a robot, a slave to what everyone expects me to be.

I may be suffering from anxiety, from anger issues and I may be a little bit insane. But if I am mentally ill and I see through all these lies, then I guess I am the one who is mentally stable.

I hear the truth behind it all. I hear the sadness and emptiness that everyone is feeling.

I try to blend in every day, but I know deep down that I am not normal, at least not for other people.

My name is Malikah, I am an *empath.*

Chapter Two
12 Years Old

I can hear her pacing around the house, talking to someone on the phone. Mom always talks on the phone; I wonder who she is so into that she keeps on going on and on for hours. I hear my dad's emotions before he even comes inside the house. He is opening the door and he feels frustrated for some reason. Why do I always hear the emotion but never what's causing it? My mother feels satisfied when she's talking to that person on the phone, but then her satisfaction turns into fear when my dad arrives. I hear her pacing into my room, so I pretend to be asleep because I have school tomorrow. She lies beside me, and I can hear not only her emotions but her breathing. She is breathing fast. Now she does not just feel fear, she feels hate. She feels like she wants to run away. She feels captured, like a bird in a cage waiting to be set free. I can smell her beautiful vanilla scent; the scent that soothes. I can feel her beautiful curly blonde hair. I wish I had curly hair like Mommy. My hair is long and brown; I think I got that from Daddy. I can hear Dad's emotions coming closer. I hear his footsteps, but his emotions are clearer for me. He opens the door and I open my eyes.

"Daddy?" I whisper in a sleepy voice.

"Malikah baby, why are you still awake?"

"I felt you coming in."

"Oh, baby I am sorry, I was looking for Mommy."

I do not answer. I don't tell him what she feels. I don't tell him that she has been ignoring him for days. I don't tell him that she is not asleep next to me, she is running. Running from something. She knows he will never hurt me, so she has chosen to sleep next to me for now.

"Go back to sleep love," Daddy tells me.

I feel his love for me, I hear it really clearly. He loves me in all the ways possible between a father and a daughter. He loves me more than Mommy ever did, and I know this because the voices tell me. The voices tell me everything.

He closes the door and leaves.

Mom opens her eyes. "I didn't know you were awake," she sighs. "I am sorry, Malikah, Mommy is tired, and she just wants time alone. Does that make sense?"

Why would that make sense to a twelve-year-old girl who is still awake at 1:00 am on a school night? It shouldn't make sense, but oddly enough it made sense to me. Not because I know the feeling, not because I have *experienced* the feeling, but because I listened to it. I understood the voices. They tell me everything.

"It makes sense to me," I finally answer. "But maybe it should make sense to Daddy too."

I never told Mommy or Daddy about the voices. I was scared that maybe they wouldn't understand, because I don't understand either. I don't know why I hear these voices; I just do.

I put my small hands on Mommy's chest, right in the middle to feel her heartbeat.

"It's okay, Mommy," I say and then I breathe deeply. And for a moment I feel like I am absorbing all the emotions she is feeling, taking it all away and exchanging it with calmness.

The voices coming from Mommy are not of fear or pain anymore. Just briefly, for a moment, she feels calm.

Did I do that?

Chapter Three
12 Years Old

It was a Thursday night when it all happened. I don't know how I can remember it so vividly, but I think it's because it changed everything.

I am trying to sleep in my room. I have turned on some cartoons to help me sleep. I don't like sleeping in the dark—it's so annoyingly silent. I hear my parents fighting outside but I try not to listen. However, I can't turn off my powers at all. I don't listen to what my parents say. I listen to what they feel. My mother is angry; she is feeling rage. My father is disappointed, and his anger is not just normal anger; he could actually break the whole house with what he feels inside.

Their voices are loud; their emotions are louder. I am scared, angry, and outraged now too. Sometimes it's hard to have emotions of my own because everything I feel is influenced by the people around me. I hear my mother screaming over and over again. I need to go out; I need to know what's going on. I am only twelve years old and I don't know what I am thinking, except that these emotions are killing me, I have to see for myself.

I stumble to reach the door. I can feel my heartbeat racing but I ignore the fear.

I go outside to see what's happening, and I freeze.

I find my father pinning my mother down on the couch. He has a belt in his hands, and he is hitting her, over and over again. His voice shocks me with every hit. I feel paralyzed.

She is screaming from the inside. I feel my heart racing even quicker; I can't breathe.

"You are the reason. You are the reason for everything bad; you need to get what you deserve. Does that hurt, Dahliah, huh? I hope it does because you have fucked up my whole life!" Daddy shouts.

"It's not my fault you are a cheating bastard. Come on, Zayne, you want to hit me, do it. That won't change shit. I'm only here for Malikah."

"Don't you dare say my daughter's name on your filthy lips."

He hits her again and she screams, "She is my daughter too."

"Oh, she never was."

They haven't seen me yet, but I fall to the ground and hit my knees.

"I can't breathe," I scream.

"Malikah," they both breathe at the same time.

"Stop, Daddy, stop. Why are you doing this?" I cry.

Dad runs to me to hold me, but I push him away. "Don't touch me with those hands."

My legs are shaking, and I can't breathe. I crawl to my mother. I hold her. She tries to hug me back, but I feel her pain. My whole body starts shaking, I feel cold.

"Mommy, I am cold."

She holds my hand and I feel her pain, her rage, and her depressed emotions.

Dad just stands there, watching me hold my mother's hand and I know he feels frustrated and betrayed for some reason. He feels pain too; he feels anger and sadness, but it all turns to anger. Only anger.

"I can't breathe," I say again as I try to inhale, exhale.

"Mommy… Daddy… I can't breathe."

"What do you mean you can't breathe?" Dad falls to the ground next to me. "Malikah, you are shaking with cold in the middle of June."

"I can't move." I feel paralyzed and cold and there is a massive pain in my chest.

"Pain, here…" I point to my chest.

I feel like I'm dying. I don't know what's happening.

I feel my father's hands wrap around me. He holds me, but then everything fades to black.

Chapter Four
12 Years Old

I wake up in a hospital bed. I don't know how much time has passed. I know that I feel sick to my stomach, and I hear voices everywhere. Voices of pain, illness, and sadness. I hate hospitals; they make my emotions even worse. I hear my mother's voices loud and clear. I know what she needs, and I am going to grant her wishes. She wants to take away the guilt. She wants to leave, without feeling the guilt of her obligations and responsibilities. I know because I feel it. I wish I didn't. I wish I lived in denial, or even like any other child my age. I wish I lived like any child waiting for parents to grant wishes. I wish I didn't have this power because all it does to me is consume me and kill me from within.

It's always a battle between what I want and feel and what others want and feel.

I know I want my mother to stay, but I know damn well she just wants to go. This is something I don't want to feel. So, I am going to let her go.

"Mommy," I call out. She comes in and I see the sadness in her eyes. I feel it too. I hear it in her voice. Oh, my sad beautiful Mommy!

"Are you okay, sweetheart?" she asks.

"Yes. But you are not."

She leans back. "Honey, don't worry—it is going to be okay."

"No, it's not," I sigh. "I know you want to leave, and actually it's your right to leave. I mean anyway who wants to live a life they do not want?"

"You think I don't want this life, here with you?"

"No, Mom, I know you don't want this life for your own reasons. I know you love me. Just not enough to stay. So go."

"Malikah, you want me to go?" I see tears in her eyes. She is crying not just because her twelve-year-old daughter is asking her to leave and be free, but because my mother, for the first time, feels like someone else understands her pain. I know she is amazed, but even though I have never told her, she has always known that I have something that others do not; superpowers that others don't own.

"Malikah, do you want me to leave?"

"It doesn't matter what I want. I just don't want someone to stay when they don't want to. I just need you to go and live your life, if you ever miss me, or want to see me, I'll be here."

I put my hand against her forehead. I inhale, I exhale, and a light is formed underneath my hand. I know I did it again, I took all these emotions, the bad ones, away.

"I love you, Mommy, go live." I break a smile.

"I love you, Malikah." And she leaves. I hear her footsteps fade. I hear her voice fade. I hear my childhood disappear.

I want her to look back. I want her to look at me, to tell me that even though things are not the best, she's going to stay for me. I want her to stay with me. To be my mother. To love me and want to be my mother, but all her emotions are not really about me, anymore. Only her, and her alone.

Oh, what a disappointment family can be.

So much for unconditional love.

My father comes into my hospital room, stunned by what has just happened.

"She left," he says in amazement. But I hear his relief.

"Yup," I answer.

"You don't care?"

"Do you want me to?"

Awkward silence falls between us for a few seconds, but he doesn't answer.

I know for a fact that my father loves my mother still, even though he denies it from the bottom of his heart. Even when he knows very well that they're beyond any fixing, even when their relationship is nothing but a disaster. I know that he loves her, even though they don't match anymore. He knows he didn't deserve her—she was his punching bag, but now she is all blown up. What I don't and will never understand is why people always deny such truth. Is it pride, ego, or terror from the ghost of too much emotion that can cause vulnerability? That drives people to hide their emotions? And not just any emotion but, supposedly, the most beautiful one of them all. Love.

Love is always denied, even when I can hear it so loud and clear. I have never seen anyone admit that it's easy. But what do I know?

I am just a twelve-year-old super-empath.

In my short life, I have heard many emotions but the weakest of them all is how people choose apathy over empathy. How people compare love to weakness. Kindness to silliness, and beauty and vulnerability to being soft and easy to break. I may be only twelve, but I feel like an adult already. Isn't it sad?

This time my emotions win. I let them win because I can't be selfish. I just want her to be happy. I just wish her happiness was with me.

Chapter Five
15 Years Old

There is nothing more depressing than being consumed by your emotions. The emotions you independently chose to leave behind. The emotions that you independently and solely decided are no good, understanding that too much emotion will make you insane. But at some point, you do realize you're absolutely insane and when that happens, it's too late. When my mother left us, everything changed. For the worse, for sure. Nothing was the same. I remember what my father told me the first day we went home to a house without a mother.

He told me that, "Despite all the bad things that have happened, I am his God-given gift." My father's emotions towards me were always full of love, but when his dictating, controlling side took over, his love changed. Throughout the years, he has convinced himself that everything he does, he does for me. Even when he is hurting me. My father's emotions have consumed him in ways that are so hard to describe. I was an adult even before I got my period. I had to absorb all the bad things he did because I knew he was hurt. I heard him. But then his hurt turned into narcissism and egotism. His needs and wants became his only priority.

He comes home late, very late. Each night with a different woman. I pretend that I am asleep, to avoid any conversation with him when he's drunk. It's hard to sleep while hearing dear father fucking some random woman in the next room. I lie down and put the pillow over my ears; sometimes I put cotton wool in them too. But nothing can erase the emotions I feel and even if the sound is blocked or not too loud after blocking my ears, I can still hear my emotions screaming out loud.

"Daddy, can you please not do the same thing tonight?" I ask, trying to avoid eye contact while pouring the milk on my cereal.

"What thing?" he says with a sleeping hangover voice.

"The women, Daddy. I hear you every night. But they magically disappear every morning."

He looks stunned for a while, like he couldn't believe that his plan to keep the women secret had failed. But at this point he really didn't care if I heard him or not.

"That's inappropriate, and none of your business to talk about," he says, also avoiding eye contact.

"I am your daughter! I shouldn't even be put in such situations." I find my voice getting loud but I'm angry.

"You've got money, a great house, beautiful branded clothes, a great international school. You basically have everything you need. So, stop bothering me now and let me do what I please."

"I need a dad, that's what I need," I tell him, trying to prevent the tears from pouring down my face. His emotions are disappointed—but not in me, in himself. I try to ignore this fact but instead of doing something about what I said, he has messed it up even more.

I know he first started doing this out of pain, but now it has become a habit and a lifestyle. I don't approve, but I guess he isn't concerned. The habit has continued and now I see some of them. Some of them stay the night. Some of them even try to befriend me.

"Your daddy is such a nice man."

"Your daddy is such a gentle man."

Of course, he is such a nice man. A man with millions of pounds in the bank, he is a nice man for all of them. He was never a nice father, or more precisely he stopped being a nice father.

I grew up hating my powers, they caused me pain. And as time went by, I suppressed them more, ignored them, and pretended that they didn't exist. At one point, I believed that

I was completely insane. Because who has the ability to hear emotions but not thought? It doesn't make sense. Why am I this way? Why me?

There are millions of questions in my mind. At a young age, my powers had no purpose, no reason but to consume the fuck out of me and kill me from the inside. It got worse when I ignored it, so like most toxic kids, I grew up to be toxic by choice. No one grabbed me, no one forced me, I went to the one thing that numbed the pain for a while, alcohol.

"Malikah, darling you can't get drunk in front of boys. It is very unattractive," my drunk, wasted father says to me, grabbing his drunk girlfriend. He will marry her by the end of the year. Ironically enough, all his wives have drunk alcohol. That must be his type. He goes around giving me advice to not get drunk, so boys won't talk about me. Because boys hate girls who drink. While he on the other hand never put down the whisky glass.

I hate when people go around giving advice like saints, but don't follow their own advice. I understand how parents want their children to behave. But don't be a fucked-up father and tell me how my life should be lived. In the end, I never told him anything after the day he completely ignored my emotions towards his actions. I stopped every true version of myself, to become the person he wanted me to be. My only companion at this point was music. Linkin Park to be precise, Chester Bennington may God rest his soul. This man saved my life too many times to count. In so many ways, I felt that he might have been an empath who chose music to help others like he helped me. Artists like Chester leave behind a legacy. Maybe one day I'll do the same but at this point in my life, there is no light at the end of the tunnel, just pretense, lies, and pain.

I started writing when I was eleven years old, the year before it all started. I have always been a sensitive child.

"It would help you to survive in the world if you toughened up a little." Father would always tell me when my emotions would take over and I could no longer control it. In some ways, he was right; in so many others, he was absolutely wrong. He never knew about my powers. My powers were my heavy secret to hold. *Writing is my art. Maybe that's how I'll save the world.*

Chapter Six
17 Years Old

I was always drunk as a teenager. I was toxic by choice. I didn't deny my emotions; my powers won't let me. I just chose to ignore them, even when it made me sick to my stomach. Drinking was my only escape; my only way out of the reality I live in. My father, however, never really noticed anything. I made sure that I grew up to be the greatest actor of all time, like any troubled teenager. I learned to pretend. But isn't that what society teaches us? To be anything we want to be, only when nobody is looking. It is okay as long as in society and with family you are the person you are expected to be. And a drunk girl always seems much worse than a drunk boy. I still don't get why, but I never really cared.

I remember sharing some emotions with this boy, the one who made the girls scream. Green eyes and tanned skin; curly hair and musical voice. At the time, I didn't give my powers credit. All I thought was that I must be insane or have some kind of sickness. I never trusted anyone enough to tell them, because who would believe a crazy drunk girl? A girl who claims she has a power? Oh, and such a lame one too. Who wants to listen to other people's true emotions? When I am barely handling my own? I was seventeen when I met this boy. I went to an excellent, expensive private school, with my cousins Noah and Karma. Me and Karma are the same age; Noah is older by one year. Although Karma and Noah are siblings, they are nothing alike.

We were at a house party at our friend Hazel's house. Hazel threw the best parties; her parents were literally never there. This boy that I called my boyfriend claimed to be so much in love with me, but I knew why. He just wanted to have sex. I heard his emotions, but I chose to get drunk instead of listening. I can't deny that I shared emotions with him but when I got older, I realized it was just the alcohol speaking. His emotions were all about himself, his sexual desires, his need to control, to own, to possess. I never knew this boy's history and never asked, but I knew he liked me enough to want to have sex with me. Sex is a sin, no one has sex without marriage but in this age, everything is changing.

I can remember all the details…

"Where the hell is Karma?" Noah asks.

I am too drunk to concentrate but I manage to say, "No idea."

Me and Noah were always closer to each other than me and Karma. Noah's emotions were all pure and genuine, unlike his ugly sister—her emotions were all jealousy, hate, and narcissism.

Hazel and Murad are sitting next to me, whispering sweet words to each other and I know for a fact, he doesn't love her. He just likes being seen with her. He likes how she is so clingy and needy, how he ignores her, but she still comes back every time. Hazel is always in denial, and no matter how badly she is being treated, she always goes back. Kind of sad for someone with a good heart to be treated in such a way. But then again, humans choose to deny the truth, and I am no different. I didn't speak my truth, I didn't tell Hazel what I knew; I didn't say anything to anyone, not even Noah. I was no different from the people I make fun of. I was also denying my truth.

I feel disgusted at the sight of Hazel and Murad, so I go to the bar to get another drink. Hazel's house is huge, and it has its own bar in the corner, underneath the marvelous huge stairs. Everyone serves themselves.

I take another glass of vodka red bull and enjoy it while looking around. People are dancing, kissing, flirting, and everybody is drinking. Many of these people are beautiful on the inside but no one really acts as they want to. Everyone is pretending to be someone else because it is hard to embrace yourself in such a fast age. Social media is taking over, and everyone wants to be special, unique, rich and… you know how it goes.

I am no different, I am a liar too. I am a liar as long as I don't speak my truth. I am a liar as long as I don't embrace my true self. But good god my true self is raw, painful, and ugly. No one likes the truth, not even me.

I start dancing and moving around; I feel my boyfriend Malek coming from behind me, to hold me around my waist. He kisses my neck and I smell his beautiful scent. His emotions, on the other hand, make me sick. I sip on my drink so I can ignore the truth. I turn to face him and let him put his hands on my hips as we dance to the music. To everyone else, we are the perfect couple; two beautiful people in love. No one knows a thing; no one suspects that this is not even close to love.

"You want to go upstairs?" he asks, and I know this sweet voice is nothing but a disguise. Boys will be boys, although not all boys are the same. Take Noah, for example. This boy has been struggling all his life for his father's acceptance and his mother's love, but though nothing works out for him, he doesn't go fuck girls randomly, or drink himself to sleep. He just tries to be better; I wish I was like Noah.

"No, not yet," I say.

I hear that his emotions are disappointed. He has asked me the same question in so many different ways. I know he wants me, but I am not sure I want the same. It's not about religion now or rules, it's more about how I feel. I feel nothing for him, and honestly, I wasn't really that drunk either.

He lets me go and excuses himself to go to the bathroom. I know he is lying; he is not going to the bathroom. So, I watch him as he moves around the crowd, trying to find his way. He is so angry; I know that for sure.

Noah comes to me and asks, "What's up?"

"Nothing, just another horny day."

"Can't take his hands off you, huh? Want me to deal with it, because I'm waiting for my cue?"

"I'm not sure it is just me he can't keep his hands off, I'm pretty sure he'll fuck the first girl who asks," I laugh and gulp the rest of my drink.

"Did you find Karma?" I ask.

"No."

"Did you look in the bedrooms?"

"Why would she be in a bedroom?"

Awkward silence falls between us. Noah's emotions suddenly burst with anger. He hasn't realized that his precious sister might be in a bedroom.

"No, she's not in a bedroom," he says in denial.

"Do you want me to come check with you?"

"Yes please," he answers immediately.

"Control your anger, Noah, I know how you feel."

"No, you don't."

"Oh, yes, I do."

We start looking around, until finally we reach the last room. Noah is losing his mind and he is too scared to witness a scene he shouldn't see.

"Let me go first," I tell him.

He looks at me as if I have saved him from the horror of expressing his ugly thoughts.

I open the door, but I know who's in there, before I go in. Their emotions are loud and clear from outside the room.

It is Karma and Malek in bed together, and oh boy did I expect this to happen.

"Malikah, what the fuck?" Karma shouts.

"Oh, you bitch," I scream.

Malek is sitting still, they are naked in bed. My boyfriend and my cousin.

Noah kicks the door open and goes towards Malek.

He pulls him down on the floor and starts hitting him, harder and harder.

"You don't mess with my family, you fuckin' man-whore."

I have never seen Noah this angry. I have never seen Noah so impulsive. But I can't lie, I enjoy seeing Malek getting what he deserves. I know it's very weird for an empath to feel like that but god damn it some people deserve a lesson or two.

Noah leaves Malek lying on the ground. Now the whole party is watching. I never loved him, but I still feel heartbroken I don't even know how. But the idea of him with Karma makes me angry. Not just because she is my cousin, but also because he is supposed to be my boyfriend.

Karma quickly puts on her dress and runs from the room, before Noah can get to her. He would never hit her; he would've just told her the truth. He would have told her she was a bitch.

And yes, Karma is a bitch.

You know what turns a genuine man to an angry, impulsive one? Betrayal and anger. Noah is a very genuine and calm person. He is a pleaser and a lover. He is so peaceful and yet here he is, hitting someone without a second thought. I don't encourage violence, but his actions were all about love. His emotions are always about pleasing and caring. Even when he was hitting Malek, his sole motive wasn't anger for the sake of anger, but anger because he believes this boy hurt me as well as his sister, and that's what moves him. Love.

That day, I decided I would tell Noah about my powers. That day, even though it was painful and ugly, I realized that someone really cared about me. That day made me realize that people like Noah exist. And the belief that good people exist makes everything possible.

Chapter Seven
20 Years Old

I am loving my new suit. My father chose it himself on his last trip to London. His wife likes to attend the fashion week there. His new wife is a stylist, so clothes are her life. My Victoria Beckham suit goes pretty well with my Dior heels. A good day today at work. This company is my legacy. It's the largest, most well-known steel company in the middle east; sister company to Hadidi real estate. My father is preparing me for the CEO position, so I can manage the company after he decides to retire.

It has been a pretty busy life since I started working with my father. I finished college two years ago. Business Management Major with straight As. I told my father that I'm not really a numbers person or a business-person, but here I am ruling a company that I will be inheriting or that will be given to me.

I go back to our penthouse. It has a stunning view, right in the heart of el Zamalek.

The house is basically like a hotel but better. I have never held a plate in the kitchen. I don't even know where the salt is kept. My father likes me that way. He wants me on fleek, spoiled and, most of all, controllable.

I have the perfect life, the perfect job, the perfect house, and the perfect future. That's what most people see when they look at me. I can't say I blame them. Everyone sees me as a spoiled daddy's girl. But they know nothing.

In my room, I change into my sweatpants and a hoodie. I put on a nice cap and let my hair hang loose around my shoulders. Wearing it up all the time gives me a constant headache.

I give my Mercedes to the parking valet and order an Uber.

I go on the stage at the Art Café , and read my poetry, and also sing a song by the person who constantly saves my life, Chester Bennington (may he rest in peace).

People here now don't call me by my name. I am known simply as "The Poet." I don't want anyone to know my name. That way, no one can go tell on me to my father.

Since I was a child, I have dreamed of being a writer. I still want to write, but there is zero chance of me pursuing my passion. Instead of facing my problems or trying to go after what I love, I lie back and pretend to be someone I am not. Then I sneak out every now and then to go read my poetry and sing songs written by the very people who inspired me to write.

My life is not perfect. I don't like brands. They are nice, yes, but they don't define me. Wearing the most expensive watch or leather jacket won't make me a better person. It won't really make me anything at all. They are a fake act, like the act I put on every day. I am not sane. I am not real. Everything happens to me and I just let it. I know I am a coward. I know my flaws; I just choose to ignore them. I am not a spoiled daddy's kid; I am simply someone who is trying to please her father.

Nothing in my life is my choice except this. Sneaking out every day, leaving my mask at home. That place. That place with its marble floors, its furniture made with rare imported African blackwood. Lilies and red roses. Fendi furniture and Versace house wear. Art collections put together by well-known Italian curators. Each and every room specified by professional designers. Yes, I live in the most amazing house, but it has no soul, no mother, no comfort, no emotions and, most of all, no peace.

In that house, I am forced to be someone else, to be not myself. Because the real me isn't acceptable.

I don't have the perfect life. But that's what people think when they look at me.

After the open mic night, I go to a bar near my house to drink some wine.

I can't be seen too much in public – I don't want people to know me – but I trust this bar, because it's been here since before I was born. No one at this bar gives a damn about me being the daughter of Zayne Al-Hadidi, the famous entrepreneur. And honestly, being his daughter shouldn't be what defines me, but here we are in a society based on looks and material things.

"Do you ever imagine a world without social levels?" I ask.

"Yeah, sure. But that's never going to happen," Noah answers and sips some of his wine.

"It would be beautiful though. Equality, no judgments, no jealousy. Many psychological disorders wouldn't even exist. If you think about it, social standards affect us all, one way or another," Sarah adds.

"You know what makes me angry? Seeing rich people do so little for others, when lower classes do so much for beggars and more," I say.

Noah and Sarah nod in agreement.

I can hear their emotions. They are always worried around me, because they are always worried *about* me. As for their emotions for each other, they are so madly in love. But they are taking it one step at a time. Every now and then they ask me what their emotional voices are telling me. And honestly, their emotions are the best part of my day. Usually, I hear fucked up emotions—especially at work. God, there is so much anger trapped inside me from being forced to work in a profession I don't like. It's killing me. But then the day ends with Noah and Sarah and everything feels alright. The voices calm down, because Noah and Sarah's emotions are calmed down. For a moment there, when I remember reciting my poetry on stage and remember people clapping for me, life seems like it has some meaning. Or it feels like maybe there is a light at the end of the tunnel. I just need to fucking dig this tunnel first. Damn light can't reach me yet.

Chapter Eight
Now 21 Years Old

Today is my 21st birthday. But everyone knows I hate my birthday, so no one really talks about it anymore. I hate my birthday because it reminds me of everything bad that has happened to me in my life. It reminds me of how lonely I am, even when I am surrounded with people. It reminds me that my mother abandoned me and that my father refuses to see me for who I am.

You can't choose your family, but you don't have to tolerate all their bad stuff either. In my case, I usually tolerate everything. Not out of weakness, but out of understanding. Sometimes even understanding can't calm you down enough to be nice or ignore what's going on, but it does help when I hear everyone's emotions and know exactly why they are acting that way. The only thing I would love to see in this world is the truth; something very rare and nearly impossible to find. No one likes the truth, no one likes it when someone is real and raw. Everyone has got so used to pretending and to being someone they're not, that eventually this fake version becomes the real version of themselves. It's hard to embrace who you are in a world full of influences. Influences that make you feel like you're not enough. I live among these people and I am telling you that they're not happy people, not real, not anything like what you see on their social media. In my case, the only thing I use social media for is to post my poems. No one knows my name. Just like in my home, if we're going to call it that. No one knows me, I only pretend to be what they need me to be.

Friday is family day, that's the tradition for almost every Egyptian family. We sit together in the alpha's penthouse. In this case, that's my father. He is the oldest of three brothers. Jabril is the middle brother; the youngest is Bilal. Dinner is served on our African blackwood table with its matching chairs. Each month, father chooses a chef to come and cook for us. This Friday, we're having A5 Kobe strip steak—Japanese beef that costs nearly $350 for 12 ounces. One of the most expensive and absolutely delicious steaks of all time.

"So, Malikah dear, why haven't you been coming to the office lately?" My father asks, sipping his vintage wine. I nearly choke at the question. I stopped going to the office because I didn't want to work with him anymore. All I really want to say to him at this point is that I am working on being a writer. But I know this will make him burst out laughing, and he'll make fun of me. Have you ever heard about any young writer living in the middle east being accepted by international agents? That's a hard equation, but I don't mind it being hard—I am going to pursue it anyway. It's my passion, I can't give up on it.

"I've been pretty occupied, lately—with my reading," I say, trying to seem casual. I am not going back to the office, but he doesn't have to know that now. Karma laughs as if I just told a joke.

"Reading about getting wasted?" she laughs.

For some reason, Karma always feels jealousy and anger towards me. I don't know if she has ever felt anything else. But her bad emotions consume her and control her. She is full of anger, loneliness and jealousy. It may be because her mother left her and Noah when she divorced their father, Jabril.

But Noah didn't turn out that way, he turned out to be a beautiful human. Despite what his parents put him through. No two people are affected the same way by anything, that's something I know. However, there is a deep light inside of everyone, that's something I strongly believe. Even inside Karma. But right now, she is a bitch. She is a genius in finance and corporate business. She has been asking for recognition all her life; she is following her father's exact footsteps. She wants to be the CFO. And one day, I'm sure she will be.

Noah, on the other hand, just likes the business. He is in charge of almost everything; he is a Co-CEO if that's even a thing. I don't understand Corporate titles. I just don't get it.

I believe Karma's constant search for recognition and appreciation from both my father and hers is the cause of her dry, soul-less ways. She doesn't care how she's going to reach her goals. She just goes for it.

"Wasted with knowledge, if that's what you mean?" Noah swoops in, trying to save the day. I look at him and smile, and he smiles back. He always has my back. My father looks at Karma disagreeably, but then looks back at me.

"Malikah isn't one to get wasted; she knows women should be elegant. Drinking too much alcohol, getting wasted is very unattractive to men. And it's also unacceptable in our society. Be careful what you joke about, Karma," he says.

I look at Karma and her eyes look at me with hate, but the dinner goes on. It is actually funny how middle eastern society still lives with such a patriarchal view of life, I don't care what people think.

I may not get wasted like I used to, but even if I did, so what? I am not here to please every walking human being on Earth. I am not perfect, why can't people realize that really no one is perfect? And that no one ever will be? It's the 21st Century for God's sake, let women do what the hell they please.

"Anyway, you must come back to the office as soon as possible; we have a new business deal on the way and Noah is managing alone. This is my legacy; disappointment is unacceptable. Being the CEO of the most well-known steel company in the middle east is no easy task."

"Our legacy," Jabril corrects.

"Yes brother, ours." My father smiles because he knows deep down that he started everything; his brothers just followed along. Except that Bilal only worked with them for two years, and then left them to open his own company offering interior design services. He expanded, and now he manufactures elegant and beautiful furniture. He is very lonely and silent. But his emotions aren't. He always feels like he doesn't belong, just like I do.

"What are you reading now?" my father asks. I am stuck now, and don't know what to say.

"Business books, about corporate business, marketing, and leadership," I improvise, trying to seem prepared and as clever as the rest of the corporate minds at the table. I wasn't going to say I am reading "Story" by Robert Mckee.

"That's interesting—but make sure you come back as soon as possible though," Father smiles. I want to break his smile, or just scream at his face and leave. But I don't, I smile back.

"Sure." I wish there was always background music playing. Music that matches how you feel, according to the moment. Right now, the song in the background would be "When I grow up" by NF. Like Chester Bennington, NF is someone who saved the world with his song lyrics. I look up to him too, he speaks the truth. One day I might actually scream at my father's face or tell him the truth about me despising the corporate world. Or maybe throw what's left of my wine in Karma's face. Or maybe just stop pretending.

Chapter Nine

"Do you like me more now?" I ask sarcastically, but Father doesn't get it.

"Oh, absolutely marvelous, isn't she?" he says, referring to the new Versace dress he bought me, that his wife chose. Wife number four in 12 years.

"Yes, darling it's a masterpiece," Tina replies. Her real name is Tahany, but she is ashamed of it because it's a really old-fashioned name. So she is known by the name "Tina." She is a perfectionist in her job, but her personality is as fucked up as he is.

"Better than the unknown dress you were wearing," my father says.

"Your taste is always so elegant, baby," Tina-the-kiss-ass tells my father.

"Oh, I couldn't have chosen the whole outfit without your help," Father replies. I, on the other hand, think I'm about to vomit now. This wife is here to stay, just the right type of kiss ass that Father likes.

"Try it on with these Dolce and Gabbana heels," Tina tells me, smiling. I feel like a Barbie doll. They dress me up the way they see fit, because apparently my style is inappropriate.

Tina doesn't love Father the way I imagine true love to be. She loves him because he has money, power, and position. She is popular and well loved, like most stylist influencers. She is 28 years old and Father is a lot older. She is young enough to be my sister. His daughter.

Her emotions aren't of hate, actually. She just wants me to leave her alone, so I do. I don't care anymore what he does, who he marries or how he chooses to fill the void inside of him. I know she uses him, but he is one of those people who likes to be used. It makes him feel like he has something that others do not have.

"Uncle Zayne?" I hear Karma calling from outside the room. She comes in and shows off her dress. "Perfection, isn't it?" she says, smiling. "Uncle Zayne how come you are so brilliant, you never fail to choose the perfect dress for every event. You are brilliant!" Karma is still smiling, another kiss ass. She kisses him then looks at me, "Oh, Malikah, that Versace dress is amazing, it is definitely way better than the shit you choose. This must be Uncle Zayne's choice, isn't it?"

Be calm, Malikah, don't break her nose just yet. I take a deep breath and slowly exhale. My father laughs, agreeing with Karma, and says, "I need you both to behave at this party. You are not children anymore. You are this company's future, so please act like it."

"You can rely on me. Malikah, on the other hand, hasn't been at work for ages." Karma is giving her puppy face, angel, good girl look.

"Well, we talked about that at dinner yesterday and I said you must come back sooner rather than later," Father says, looking at me. We actually talked about nothing. He talked, and then replied to himself. He doesn't understand the idea of a conversation; that it has to be two ways. In his case, conversation is him saying what he wants, stating his orders and then expecting puppets like me to obey. "You must come back to work tomorrow after this party. There will be no more excuses, I don't care what they hell you're doing." I can hear Karma smiling inside.

"We work all day and you sit on your ass all day, doing nothing," Karma says, trying to hide her smile. Her emotions are loud, clear, full of jealousy and hate. Full of a love of power and superiority. She is a true Hadidi; full of fucked up beliefs and excessive self-love.

"Karma, watch your language," my father says and then turns to me. "Karma has indeed been doing great work, but Malikah you need to come back and manage everything."

"Aren't I doing a good job, Uncle Zayne?" Karma asks, again pulling her angel face.

"Yes, darling, you are. But Malikah is the next CEO, and you are the next CFO. So Malikah should be equally involved, if not much more so."

Karma doesn't like the fact that she is only the CFO. If it was in her power, she would kick me out and be the ruler of the Hadidi empire. She knows she can't just do this though, so she works hard, hoping to be considered as important as me.

"I learned from the best," Karma says, hugging Father. "I can't wait to nail this business deal." Still smiling, she spitefully looks me up and down and then leaves.

I am still trying to calm down. I don't want to get angry, or my panic attacks might take over.

"Have you ever considered the fact that maybe I have my own passion?" I finally manage to ask Father but, as expected, he completely ignores me.

"Be ready for the party. Come to work tomorrow. It's not a choice, Malikah. I have been so easy on you. Please stop acting like a child. My face is in the fucking dirt because of you. Look at Karma behaving like a true Hadidi. She comes to work, prepares for business deals and important parties. I will not tolerate any more of your irresponsible ways. Now leave."

I look at him in disbelief. I don't know why, because I expected this answer. I guess I still hope for something different. In this moment, the song *Only* by NF would be a great backing track.

I go back to my room and find Noah still on the bed where I left him. I change into sweatpants and a hoodie and lie down next to him.

"Did he bring up work again?" Noah asks.

"Yes. This time was quite intense, and I felt visible threats in his voice," I sigh. "Apparently his face is also in the dirt because I am irresponsible."

"That's a new one."

Noah's emotions are always worried about me. His emotions are full of love and care. Even though he works in the family business, he doesn't let that corrupt him in any way. He definitely has a temper when anything happens to one of his loved ones. But he is one of those rare people whose emotions are true and genuine.

"You know, Malikah, when you finish your book and find an agent, this will change. He might actually let you be whatever you please."

"He won't be happy, because I am not what he wants me to be."

"Well, when it happens, it won't matter what he wants, will it?" He hugs me and we hear a knock on the door.

"Oh, no hugging without me, I want in!" Sarah, my best friend and also Noah's girlfriend, jumps in to join the hug.

"It's going to be alright," Noah tells me. And even though it doesn't seem like it, the way he says it makes me feel like maybe I can believe him.

Chapter Ten

I'm wearing the Versace dress that Father and Tina chose for me. I have straightened my long, silky brown hair and put on some simple makeup. Sarah insisted I should also put on lashes. It's hard to argue with her when she gives you her puppy eyes. Sarah was a psychology major in college, she is pretty much a genius. For some reason, she also loves makeup so much. She always says that if she wasn't a psychologist, she'd be a make-up artist. Noah and I laugh when she says this, because we have no clue how those two things go together.

"You're all done," Sarah says.

"Finally! God, I feel like I have been sitting here for ages. You'd make a great make-up artist doctor," I tell her.

Sarah looks at me and pouts. "Come on, you look beautiful. And yes, I'd make a great make-up artist."

"Was I not beautiful before?"

"Don't pull that one, my Malikah Zayne," she smiles. "You're beautiful all the time."

Noah comes into the room. "Wow, what have you done with Malikah? Are those lashes? Oh MY GOD!" he bursts out laughing.

"What's wrong? Women like lashes." Sarah looks at him and frowns.

"Yea, sweetie, women like them—not Malikah."

I laugh because I know what he means. I have always been a tom boy, but I can't deny that I like dresses. Lashes are normally a bit too much for me but well, I like them so far.

"I actually like them," I tell him.

"Well, great! You both look gorgeous." Noah hugs Sarah and kisses her cheek.

I feel like I want to take a picture of this moment. These two people who genuinely love each other. Their emotions sing with love and passion whenever they are in the same room. In a few minutes, at the party, I will have to meet people that I don't get along with. But knowing that love and passion like this exist makes me feel like this world still has some good in it.

"Time to network," Noah says, excited for the business deal waiting to be closed.

"Oh, time to go to hell you mean," I reply, frowning.

He smiles and hugs me. "Make some notes for your book, how about that?"

"I was actually thinking about it."

"Perfect, then we're good to go."

Father comes slamming through the door and asks, "What the hell are you still doing here? The party started an hour ago. Malikah, I need to speak to you in a bit." Then he leaves.

We all look at each other. But really, they are looking at me. They are worried that I might do something crazy tonight. They are worried things will go up in flames. But I'll try not to do that for them. I don't like it when they are worried, however, they worry all the time. They love me so much, sometimes too much, and definitely more than I deserve. I don't even understand why such great people tolerate a mess like me, but they do.

"Okay, you heard the man, let's go," Noah says, trying to maintain his everlasting enthusiasm.

Put on a happy face, Malikah, I tell myself.

There are people all over the penthouse—celebrities, business tycoons, and evidence of way too many plastic surgeries. Millions of dollars under one roof, and no one is worthy, that's the irony. Money doesn't determine anything—not your personality, or how good a person you are, not your beauty or how human you are. If anything, most people—if not all of them—are changed when money is involved. Throughout history, money, power, and sex have been the ultimate motivations for humans. Not emotions, not doing the right thing, not peace. But like anything, it differs from one person to another. Once again, I'll take Noah as an example; born rich and beautiful with his dark brown hair, hazel eyes, and tanned skin. He is more human than anyone else in this room will ever be. I wander around, clutching a glass of wine, and try to avoid conversations. They treat me so nicely, the daughter of Zayne AL-Hadidi. How can they not be nice? I hate that.

"Malikah, honey, come here. I want to introduce you to someone," Father calls me over.

"Sure," I reply, almost choking.

"Mr. Maged, this is my daughter Malikah Zayne AL-Hadidi," Father announces with a flourish.

Did you really have to say my full name? Ugh.

"Oh, they grow up so fast, don't they?" Mr. Maged kisses both my cheeks. "Darling, you look beautiful."

"Thank you," I say with a great smile on my face. This is my diplomatic face. I'm hoping this party will end well.

"This is my oldest son, Nadeem," Mr. Maged tells me.

Oh, I see where this is going now. *Don't explode yet, Malikah.* The emotions I am hearing from all around the room are making me sicker by the minute. But I am trying to maintain my diplomatic face.

Light brown hair, dark brown eyes, a sculptured jaw, and beautiful smile. Not such beautiful emotions though. He is standing in front of me.

"Hello, Nadeem." We shake hands.

"Hello, Malikah."

I immediately hear his emotions screaming hard. He finds me attractive. So I play along, still maintaining the diplomatic face.

My father says, "So, Malikah, why don't you show Nadeem around? Me and Maged have some business talks to finish. You guys go have fun." My father looks at me and smiles. I want to break that smile. I know what he is thinking. These two fathers—mine, and Nadeem's—are setting us up together. Like any wealthy family in Egypt, if not in the world, fathers want to choose who their kids will marry. To make sure they blend with a family with the same standards. And it's even better when the parents are business partners.

"Well, let's go, Nadeem."

"Right after you," he replies, smiling. Any normal woman would melt at this smile. But I know what's behind it. He's his daddy's puppet with no actual independent personality. Just like I pretend to be in front of people. But he is actually like that.

I show him around while gulping one glass of wine after another. We reach my favorite place, the roof.

"Oh God, it is so beautiful up here," Nadeem tells me. "We live in the suburbs, so don't really have a view. We have a huge garden though, but roofs are much better." Nadeem watches as I drink my fourth glass of wine.

"Uh-huh, yeah I get you," I say without looking at him. He doesn't know that I stand up on this very fence looking down, trying to find it in me to jump. I'll let him enjoy the view.

"You drink a lot."

I look at him and frown. "Is that a problem?"

"No, just that it's not very healthy."

"You're holding your second glass of whisky, telling me I am not healthy?"

"I mean…" he starts to reply, but I cut him off.

"…it is not healthy for a girl?"

"No, I don't mind girls drinking."

"You shouldn't."

"I was just trying to make conversation," he says and I hear his frustration.

"Okay," I sigh. "Look, Nadeem, me and you will never happen. I don't know what your father told you, or what conversation you're going to have after the party."

"Don't you find me attractive?"

"Oh God, no, it's not that. You are very attractive," I tell him, smiling.

"So, why not?"

"Because I don't want to be part of a business marriage. That's not who I am. And do you actually want to know the truth?"

"Yes, please."

"You are a daddy's boy. You are his puppet. I don't care how wealthy or how beautiful you are. I don't give a fuck if you drink, fuck, or smoke. But I wouldn't accept a man being too much of a daddy's boy. You are just trying to make him proud. You deny yourself by hiding in his shadow. I know you don't want that either. You are a liar, a self-centered, spoiled boy. It is all his fault though—he didn't raise you to be independent, but it's okay. Just a little piece of advice, I wasn't raised to be the way I am, Father thinks I am a spoiled child too, but no one really knows me." I finish the last sip in my glass.

"What the hell are you saying?"

"You know that I'm right. Do you really want this, or do you want to open your own business, find love with a woman who loves you back? And for once just be who you want to be, without your father's permission. Be the man you really hoped you'd grow up to be."

Nadeem stands in front of me, stunned. He knows what I have said is true, but it has never been said to his face before. All he has ever tried to do is imitate his father, be the good kid and obey orders. Being his own individual person doesn't really apply, because fathers always rule their children. They shape them and create the version they want. Some rebel, like I did, while maintaining the image their fathers want. Some surrender, like Nadeem, and become exactly what their parents want.

"Where are you going?" Nadeem grabs my hands and I know now that he is not attracted to me just because of my looks, but also because I light up a place inside him. A place he has been ignoring.

"Out, this party is lame," I say.

"But your father…"

"He won't notice."

He lets go of my hands. I feel his thoughts eating him, so before I go, I smile and tell him to find somewhere away from everybody else.

"That's the only way." I smile again and this time he smiles back.

I change into my sweatpants and hoodie and sneak out of the penthouse to take a walk. I text Noah that I am going to Cairo Cellar, a bar near the penthouse.

I take a walk along the streets, it's 11pm on a Saturday night.

I walk and look around; I am not that drunk yet. I hear people's emotions on the streets. They all contradict, but they all share the same thing; fake happiness. I find a woman and her child, walking. The woman is pretty occupied with her phone call and is pulling the little kid along so fast that his small legs can't keep up. The child is frustrated and starts to cry, but the woman isn't even aware that he is upset. She is talking to someone she likes, probably a boyfriend. I stand in front of the woman as she tries to pass.

"Stop," I say.

She looks at me, disagreeably. I take a Patchi chocolate from my pocket, and hand it to the little boy, smiling.

He smiles back and says, "Thank you."

"You are welcome, dear," I tell him.

I look at the woman and she looks back at me in amazement.

"You have a child, act like it. Be responsible. He can't keep up with you walking at that speed. You were so occupied with your phone call, you didn't even notice him crying."

The woman is stunned for a second.

"Who the hell are you to tell me how to treat my child?" she demands.

"I am the emotions that humans leave behind," I tell her as I walk away.

I feel her emotions – she is surprised, angry, and irritated by what I just did, but she bends down and picks up her child, watching him enjoy the chocolate. The child leans sleepily on his mommy's shoulders, and finally feels secure. That's what

I wanted to see. The woman didn't argue with me, because I told her what she needed to hear. She knew she was being careless, so when I pointed it out, she just accepted it. Sometimes people just need a push to realize their feelings, and the side effects that their actions have on others.

I keep walking towards the Cairo Cellar and find couples holding hands. I know exactly which ones really love each other, and which ones are just in it for the fun. It's sad how relationships are sometimes so fucked up that a person in love is incapable of recognizing a toxic relationship. We all deny the truth when we love someone, but we don't realize how much it affects us. It destroys us from the inside, until there is nothing left for us but to realize what we have done. Love should be pure and genuine, but humans twist it, distort it, and turn it into this ugly thing that these days we call "fear of commitment." It's so sad, turning beauty into such ugliness.

I look around and I see beggars everywhere. Some of them are actually in need, some of them are just begging for money. Either way it's sad. Every day I witness little children wiping cars for money, selling tissues in traffic, or I see mothers with children on every street begging for money. I try to imagine a world with no social standards, where money isn't the thing that determines humans needs and satisfaction, where love is the real wealth and emotions are blunt and clear. A world where there is equality not just in gender, or in race but in standards. In the end a rich woman is treated better than a poor one. A rich man is treated better than a poor one. Poor people feel compassion for the poor, because they are going through the same thing. While the wealthiest men and women on Earth do so little for them, even when they have the money for it.

If I was in control of my father's money, I'd build a house for the homeless. I'd help them out if they let me. If I could change this world, I'd tell everyone the truth behind their pain and teach them to realize it on their own. The thing that remains constant throughout my life is that even when I deny my powers and my true self, deep down I know exactly who I am. Sometimes I hate myself for all the times I did people wrong, all the times I said the wrong things at the wrong times, all the times I hurt people with truth because I was so angry. Sometimes I hate myself because I feel like I am not good enough, not for the life father wants me to live, nor the life I wish to live but that I still have no clue how to achieve.

Hating myself won't get me anywhere, that's for sure, so I try to accept myself. But how can I accept myself when I hear pain, anger, need, and sadness and do nothing about it? Noah is always telling me that I can't save the world. But how come my favorite heroes saved me; Chester Bennington, NF, Matt Haig, Leonardo da Vinci, and Charles Bukowski. Different artists from different ages and different professions have saved me, each in a different way. I know there will never be equality but there will always be Art. Art makes you feel like you belong, even when everything around you makes you feel like you don't.

I reach the pub and go inside. It is empty, just the way I like it. Only one other guy is there, sitting alone in the dark. I sit at my normal table, right beside the bar and he's sitting on the other side of the room. I can feel his eyes on me while I order a jug of red wine Sangria – a whole jug, just for me.

I don't hear his emotions, that's weird!

I try to listen up close, I am not that drunk. And actually when I *am* drunk, I can still hear emotions – they are just a bit distorted.

I pour my first cup of sangria and drink it, sip by sip. I love it but I can't concentrate because I am very concerned as to why the hell I can't listen to that boy's emotions.

He stands up and comes my way. His face becomes clearer as he approaches me. Short, dark curly hair, light brown or hazel eyes. I can't really tell what color they are. He is tall, and handsome. His lips are full, and his body looks athletic and fit.

"Hello," he says, eyeing me.

His eyes are a light shade of walnut.

"Hello," I reply.

He grabs a chair and sits down. Now that's creepy and inappropriate, but I let him.

"Who are you?"

"Me? You're the one sitting at my table."

He looks at me for a moment and then asks, "Why can't I hear anything from you? Do you hear anything, or is it just me?"

My heart is beating fast and I feel myself sweating; my anxiety is kicking in. What the hell is he saying? Is he like me? Am I not the only one? Or is this a game? Is he a liar, is he pretending? I can't hear anything; this is confusing and irritating. I never thought it would feel this weird, not being able to hear someone's emotions. What am I supposed to do now? I feel my heart racing.

"Excuse me, I have to go." I stand up, leave the money for the sangria on the table, and run to the door.

He follows me.

Chapter Eleven

He follows me outside, and now I am getting scared. Because who does that? I feel my anxiety rising, and I don't know if it's because a creepy stranger is following me, or if it's because I can't hear this creepy stranger's emotions. I know for a fact that if he is anything like me, then that's making him anxious, driving him crazy too.

"I am not trying to scare you. I don't usually do this, but you've got to know what I am talking about, otherwise why would you run away?" he calls out after me.

I don't stop. I can't. So, instead of thinking about what he's just said, I scream, "Stop following me." And I keep walking quickly toward the penthouse. I text Noah to come meet me halfway. The guy is still following me.

He overtakes, and stops right in front of me, forcing me to stop. I freeze.

"Look, I came to the pub today feeling ugly and hopeless," he sighs, looking at me. "I don't know if you understand me, or if it's even okay to pour myself out in front of a complete stranger. Let me at least walk with you."

"Well, you already invaded my alone time, thank you so much. You are bothering me even more than I was already bothered," I say, my face not giving anything away.

"I am not crazy," he replies. "I think you know exactly what I mean."

"No, I don't." But why am I even arguing? I know exactly what he means.

"Don't lie. I might not hear your emotions, but I know that lies don't hide. Just tell me, who are you?"

"Me? Who the fuck are you?" And now I'm angry. Is that because I know what he means but can't admit it? Now I am confusing my own emotions.

"I am emotions," he tells me with a very straight, emotional, and deeply sensitive look in his eyes. I watch him breathe heavily as he speaks these three words. He is anxious too—although I can see it but not hear it. His eyes are bright, and now they look more hazel than walnut. I look at him for a moment, unable to answer. Ironically, my breath is lost among all the burning questions inside of me too.

He doesn't take his eyes off mine. I have never looked at someone for so long, so deeply. His voice softens and he asks, "So just tell me, do you hear my emotions?"

I stop walking and look back at him. "No," I whisper, breathing deeply. Trying to manage my anxiety. Hearing emotions makes me anxious, and now it seems that not hearing them makes me anxious too. *Nice one*, I say to myself sarcastically.

"Me neither. I thought I was the only one." He comes closer and introduces himself.

"My name is Adam."

Well, Adam, you are an extremely attractive man that I am going to run away from anyway, I think to myself. I sigh, his eyes are so beautiful, so full of emotions that I can't hear. I stand there for what feels like forever. He looks deep into my eyes as if he is looking directly at my soul. Weirdly, I feel like I am looking directly at his soul too. It feels like time simply stands still.

We are silent, and everything is calm. We're the only ones on the street, under the dim lights. A few cars pass by, but it doesn't cut into the calmness I feel. For some reason, I hope that he is feeling the same. As we stand there, looking into each other's eyes, I feel my anxiety fading. He doesn't take my breath away; he makes me breathe. And all I can think about now is how much I want to know him.

"Malikah!" I hear Noah shouting and see him running towards me.

"Your name is Malikah," Adam smiles. His smile is childlike and pure. I am sure he doesn't know it. I love his smile already, but I don't let on. I maintain my poker face.

"Who the hell are you? Stop following my cousin," Noah shouts at him.

I stop him. "Noah, wait, he is like me."

"What do you mean, like you?" Noah breathes heavily. He has been running, feeling anger and worry.

"Calm down, Noah, it's okay," I tell him. "Breathe."

"You said there was someone following you—but now you're telling me he is like you? What the hell does that mean?"

"It means we have the same powers," Adam tells him.

Noah looks at him, then back at me and whispers, "What? Is that even possible?"

"Well, according to neuroscience, it's possible but very rare," Adam says.

"I wasn't asking you, smart ass." Noah glares at him angrily and then looks back at me. "What does this mean, Malikah?"

"It means I am not the only one." I break into a smile, not knowing if that's a good thing or not. I know Noah will feel over-protective of me, because that's how he has always been.

I give Adam my phone, "Write your phone number here."

"Okay," he says. "I'll be waiting for you."

I look at him one more time. I dive deep into his hazel, walnut color-changing eyes. But it's only a quick dive because now he is leaving. I know I can't hear his emotions, but I know he is as curious as I am.

Noah and I walk back to the penthouse in silence. We don't utter a single word. Trying to let this new knowledge sink in.

"Okay look, you need to be careful," Noah says eventually.

"I didn't hear his emotions, Noah. That's proof enough that he is like me. For some reason, we don't hear each other's emotions. Maybe our powers fight each other. I don't know, I just know that this guy is like me, Noah. Do you know what that means?" I ask passionately. And I feel it in me. I want to know him; I want to know more.

Noah sighs, "You were never alone, Malikah."

"No, Noah, I was never alone physically. But in my mind, it's killing me. Each minute that passes I just want to explode."

"Just be careful."

"I will."

I don't know what to expect. I just know that if there is one person like me, there might be more. And if there are only two of us, then there must be a way to control these powers or at least to manage them. Adam seemed frustrated, yes. But he also seemed contained. He looks like someone who knows so much, and I would like to know too. I would like to know it all.

I am trying not to get my hopes up because I'm so used to getting frustrated. But for some reason, this guy… Adam, feels like hope in a human form.

Chapter Twelve

I was hoping that Father wouldn't catch me sneaking back in, but he has. He shouts about how irresponsible I am to take a walk in the middle of the night, when I clearly should have been there for the party.

"We'll discuss your irresponsible behavior later, now go get dressed and burn those sweatpants of yours. God! What a mess," he yells as he leaves the room. At this moment I would normally have felt angry, but my mind is very occupied with Adam and his color-changing eyes. Noah takes me to my room so I can get changed. I have got to admit that I am tipsy but not yet drunk.

"He wants me to marry this guy Nadeem, it's too obvious, Noah, I am telling you," I tell him angrily.

"Oh God, your father is getting worse and worse. But hey, my father finally gave up on me!" he laughs. Noah's father Jabril is such a pain in the ass. Noah is better, wiser, and much more knowledgeable than him. Noah chose to work for the company because he likes the business, but his father wants him to follow his footsteps in the world of numbers and finance like Karma. Noah's strengths have always been his diplomacy and creativity. He will lead this company to places that it wouldn't go without him. The funny part is, Jabril actually got jealous of him. But now, he leaves Noah alone.

Noah assures me that nothing will happen against my will as long as he is alive.

"I mean, he has done enough," he says, referring to my father. "Want to tell me what happened with that guy?" Noah sees that I am still shocked and panicked, and yet very curious.

I tell him all about it—from the moment I stepped into Cairo Cellar to the moment he came running for me. I see his expression changing as well. We never thought there was anybody else like me. If there is one, then there could be more. But if there aren't any more people like us, and we're the only ones, then what does that mean? We don't have much time to discuss any hopes, dreams, or assumptions. We have to get back to the party. This time, I'm the funny, charming, loving CEO daughter Malikah. I don't want trouble with the Alpha (AKA my father), I just want the day to be over.

I drink one last glass of wine to be just a little bit more than tipsy, and I now I'm on fire. Networking, talking, chatting, making jokes, and friendly with absolutely everyone. Oh, Father's eyes are so proud to see this side of me—it's all he's ever wanted. I try not to get too drunk, but still maintain a certain amount of alcohol, so that I can tolerate the fucked-up emotions everywhere in the crowed. After the party I finally have the freedom to be Malikah again. Father comes over to me. He is so proud—I can see it but, more importantly, I can hear it too.

"Well, you did a great job," Father tells me as I take off my heels. They have been killing me all night.

"Thanks, but this party is not for me, I am not a part of it. Plus, this Nadeem guy? Never going to happen," I find myself saying. Normally I would think twice before speaking like this—trying to avoid arguments.

"Well, this family, this company, and this life is not yours to choose. You are a part of it whether you like it or not. This is what I am leaving behind. You can't disappoint me. It's unacceptable." He pauses and then says, "And Nadeem is not a must, we'll find someone you like."

I want to hit him in the face. I want love, I want emotions, I want freedom of choice. Not a fucking man-boy.

"And the clothes you were wearing before? Throw them in the trash. My daughter only wears brands and obviously they weren't brands. They looked ugly."

You look ugly from the inside, I think to myself.

"We have a meeting tomorrow at 10am. Be there. If you hadn't charmed the whole party, I would've been in a very different mood now. I am so proud you have the CEO DNA in your blood."

Oh God no, you mean I have the actress DNA in my blood. I keep quiet because having a conversation with him is impossible. He only listens to what he says, he never listens to others. His ideas and thoughts are always brilliant, no matter how mediocre. Everyone else is stupid and undereducated. Now I am left here with the knowledge that I will never be able to choose my path in life. I will never be able to figure out who I am for real. I will never get away from this control freak of a father.

I go to my room to find Sarah wearing some of my pajamas, sitting on my bed.

"I think those heels have broken my leg. I can't feel my toes."

After everything that has happened tonight, I laugh my heart out because her expression is priceless. And more importantly because I know that even in the darkest of places, there has got to be light.

I tell her about the night that I've had, and about the fact that I will never be able to figure myself out. Sarah is not much of a talker; she is a psychologist. She listens and lets people figure it out through offering them simple key words or questions. However, with me she doesn't talk, she just feels, and I listen.

She hugs me tight and says, "I believe in you. I know it doesn't seem like it, but you'll find your way. You just have to be brave enough to accept some losses and be resilient enough to go down the path anyway."

Sarah lost her father when she was just thirteen. Her mother took care of her but then she got sick with heart disease. I can't even spell the disease that she has. Despite all this, Sarah never gave up on her dream. She kept studying in college to be a psychologist and became a valedictorian. She is a genius in what she does. I don't believe in formal education that much; some people are stupid even though they go to college. But I believe in passion—in this case Sarah's passion for psychology and research. She takes care of her mother and works to provide for her. She has applied for a scholarship that I am sure she'll get, to travel and complete her Master's degree in London. She's planning on taking her mother with her, to get her the best treatments. Sarah is an example of a determined, passionate person.

I don't know if I am brave enough to pursue what I love, or even if the world will let me do it. Sarah always says that to get to where we want to go, we will lose a lot along the way. But when we get there it will be worth it.

The thing is, I don't know if I am worth it, or if I am brave enough to break free.

Chapter Thirteen
18 Years Old

Love and sex comes along right. Some people mistake one for the other. In my country, and, in fact, in all the Arab countries, a girl who is not a virgin is unworthy. She is used property. Love is such a divine, inexplicable feeling when it's true. But even more than other corrupted emotions in our generation, love has been corrupted the most. You'd say it's easy for me to know real love from fake love, but it doesn't work that way. When I fall in love, even I become completely blind.

The first and only time I actually fell in love, I was 18 years old. He was 21. Let me tell you about relationships in middle eastern countries; the man gets away with ANYTHING. The woman is basically there to care, nurture, love, give, and be completely open. If she stops being any of these things, then she is irresponsible, unreliable, and doesn't fulfill her duties as a woman. A woman can't make mistakes, complain, or even argue too much because then she'd be a very negative person. On the other hand, men are big babies with toys. And that never changes, even when cultures develop, technologies develop, even when the whole damn world develops. Men are still big babies with big toys and unfortunately women are considered their property.

But Ramy, I thought he was different. Don't we all think that in the beginning? He was loving, loyal, funny, and absolutely beautiful. He made me feel less sick than anybody else. It was my first year of college and his last. Of course, I was forced by my dear father to apply for a business major, and that's how we met.

He was charming, the type of man girls look at in the street. Light brown hair, green eyes, and an absolutely smoldering smile. Of course, I fell for him like the others, and I knew that I loved him more than he ever loved me.

"This is a nice restaurant," I said, smiling so hard that my face hurt.

"Yes, isn't it? I thought we should celebrate."

"Celebrate what?"

"Well, you being in my life is enough to celebrate, isn't it? Plus it's our five month anniversary," he said, giving me the smile that melts everyone away. But it felt wrong. The voices told me he was lying, that we were celebrating for a different reason, but I smiled anyway. He always said the right things. He always knew what to say, and when to say it. He gave a great first impression, but he was never what he claimed to be.

It was such a lovely night, the night I gave myself to the wrong person.

"Do you want to go back to my place and relax for a bit?" he asked with lust in his eyes.

"Yes, sure, why not?" I knew it wasn't love. I knew it was lust. But I went anyway.

We went to his house. He was still living with his parents, because in the middle east, children do not move out until they're married. Such a stupid concept.

We lay on his bed. I was wearing a short black dress. He'd taken off my fur coat when we arrived.

He started kissing me more and more, and it was fine. But then he put his hand on my inner thigh, sliding it higher with each kiss. He started forcing himself on me.

"Wait, wait!" I cried out, in panic.

"Well, I thought it would be a nice night to… you know."

"No, I don't know."

"Have sex," he said, smoldering his smile at me.

"We can't, Ramy. For starters, it's inappropriate. And in any case, you should've asked me first."

He got up, anger washing over him.

"Ask you?" he laughed sarcastically. "I am trying to show you how much I love you, and you are telling me to ask you? This is my way of showing love and you are rejecting me. Very nice."

He felt angry, did I mistake his feelings? Was it love or lust, I couldn't tell because I was panicking. Was he leaving me? The only person who I let into my life was leaving me. I couldn't let that happen.

"No, baby, I didn't mean it that way. I just thought this should be special," I said, giving him my best puppy eyes.

"Well, what's more special than a five month anniversary? I thought you'd be happy." He left his room. I heard him turn on the TV and I sat on the bed, not knowing what to do.

At the time, I didn't realize he was manipulating me into doing what he wanted. Even though the emotions coming out of him made me feel sick, I followed him to the living room anyway.

"Okay, let's do it," I said, forcing a smile. "Please don't leave me."

He stood up and hugged me. "I can never leave you. Don't you know I love you? I told you Malikah, I'll wait till you finish college so I can marry you as soon as you do. How come I am planning our future and yet you still don't trust me?"

The emotions told me that he loved me, but not the way I loved him. I knew there was something weird, something I didn't yet understand. I just wanted him to stay. If doing this would make him stay, if doing this would make him love me more, then fine.

I started kissing him and he kissed me back, harder.

He slid his hands down my back, till he reached my ass and grabbed it hard.

I felt pain, but not just physical. I felt pain in my stomach, my heart, my head, and my emotions.

I let him touch me and I knew I didn't want him to.

He started kissing me more, undressing me at the same time. He ripped my dress.

It's okay, he loves you, Malikah, I told myself.

He threw me on the couch and pulled off my lace socks. I let him do it.

He loves you, Malikah, it's okay.

He kept kissing and biting and kissing. I felt breathless, hated the feeling of his lips on my body.

With no hesitation, warning, or even one bit of intimacy he thrust himself inside me, and I screamed.

"Yes, baby, say my name."

I felt the tears in my eyes and tried not to let them pour down my face.

This wasn't sex, or rape. It was a mix of both. He didn't care if I was even turned on. He didn't care if I wanted it. He had manipulated me, and I had believed him. Stupid me. I didn't listen to the voices, and I had been too drunk to realize. Although it wouldn't have made a difference, I loved him too much to care about the truth.

I gave in to him, because I thought I loved him, because I thought he loved me. I gave in because I wanted to show him that I loved him, even more than he loved me. But apparently it doesn't work that way.

After that we kept having sex, lots of it. I got used to it, but I never really enjoyed it. People say it's one of the most intimate connections, but in my case it was a one-way road. He'd come and come again, never asking me if I was okay, or if I liked it. He liked me to be submissive and follow exactly what he wanted me to do. In many ways I knew I was forced into it, but I was scared that I might lose him if I didn't please him enough.

I am a pleaser and I loved him, I wanted him all for me and me for him. I didn't realize until much later that I had been forced into it.

After that night sex became the only reason we met. We stopped going out on dates. We stopped talking. All we did was have sex and when I complained, he just got angry.

"What the hell, Malikah, we are hanging out."

"No, we're just having sex over and over. Don't get me wrong, I love having sex with you," I lied. "But not when it's the only reason we meet."

The voices warned me about his anger and his controlling ways. It was like I was in love with a younger version of my father. I wasn't his girl, or his baby anymore. I was his property, and his possession. And when I realized that…everything changed.

"You are immature and can't hold a conversation unless its solely for your own benefit. You don't love me; you only love yourself. You worship your needs. You knew that me having sex with you would tie me to you, because our society makes it unacceptable. But you know what? I don't give a fuck, because I would rather spend my whole life alone than be anywhere near you." I started laughing hysterically. "You know, Ramy, I have superpowers."

"You're drunk."

"No, I am not, I can listen to emotions. Do you want to know your truth?"

He looked a bit freaked out but was still curious.

"You are a self-centered man You wanted to have sex with me from day one. This wasn't love. Yes, you have got some emotions but not that many, and definitely not like the ones I had for you."

"Had?" he asked.

"You love yourself too much to look out for other people's emotions. My reaction is freaking you out. I wonder why? Maybe it's because my father is such a powerful man and he would actually kill you if he knew. Or maybe it's because you know deep down that you don't love me, and you think I'm just a crazy person. You are a control freak and a liar." I paused.

"I never enjoyed sex with you. You practically raped me. I never orgasmed. I never enjoyed it. You have fucked up the whole concept of sex in my fucking head."

"Raped you? I love you, Malikah. What are you talking about?"

I feel his fear, his hidden anger.

"LIAR, LIAR, LIAR, LIAR," I screamed to his face.

"You are insane," he said.

"You don't care, you just wanted sex out of this, didn't you? And I actually denied my emotions and my powers. I thought you loved me, now you make me feel sick." I laughed some more but could feel my tears screaming to be let out. I held them in because I was not going to cry in front of an asshole like him.

"You are such an insecure person, you fear being alone so much it kills you. You fear being judged and you are too obsessed with your looks because you think they define you. You are insecure about how people see you – and that's why you know so much about giving a great first impression. But if someone asks you about anything, you are actually clueless because you are not as knowledgeable or as wise as you fucking claim to be. You are a man-boy seeking acceptance from a fucked-up society like everyone else. You thought you'd imprison me and own me if you made me an un-virgin. Well, guess what? I don't give a damn."

I heard his anxiety, but it didn't stop me.

I kept going on and on about his lies, and his insecurities. I left that day and we never saw each other after that. He had used me, used my money, used my family, used everything for his own benefit. He lied and lied only to seek acceptance. He wasn't true, or loyal and his beautiful face turned ugly when I realized the truth about him, when I listened to my emotions. Ramy moved away from college that year, after I exposed him to himself. People doesn't like it when truth is laid raw and ugly in front of them, especially when it's a truth about themselves. People freak out when I tell them the truth, and Ramy freaked out even more because I got too deep into his insecurities. He freaked out because of my powers. So I decided it's not worth telling people, it's better to remain the ambiguous girl that no one knows anything about.

The realization that I was being used hurt me deep down. It made me feel like maybe people are just always that bad. Noah didn't know about what had happened with Ramy until a year later, and even then I didn't tell him we had sex because he would have freaked out. He probably would have wanted to kill the guy, as he has always seen me as a twelve-year-old who needs protection. The way my anger exploded at Ramy made me realize how much I was holding back. I am dangerous to humankind. I am emotions, truth, and reality. Humans don't like any of these three when they're blunt and raw.

I grew up like most girls, wanting to please the men in my life, starting with Father. This time I spent with Ramy was the only time I felt brave enough to not care if I pleased my father or not. I was forced into sex, but I had rearranged my thoughts and tricked myself into believing it was out of love. Ramy made me feel like this is what love is. I ignored my powers. Instead, I pleased a man and forgot all about myself. The relationship turned me into a slave to his needs and I will never be like that again. No matter how much time goes by, and no matter how strong the feminist movement grows, men still think their needs are the center of the universe. All women come to realize this at some point in their lives. And when a woman breaks down like I did, we make sure not to give all our hearts ever again.

I guess in many ways, people like to be manipulated, or rather accept manipulation. Empaths know the truth and despite that, they still let themselves be manipulated because they don't want to accept the truth. I let him do that. But no more.

Chapter Fourteen
Now

I grow more outraged at the world. But even outraged and hungover, I still wake up and take a shower to attend my father's compulsory meeting. The thing with pleasing Father is that it's not optional because if you disobey, he'd probably destroy your life. I take a look at my reflection in the mirror after a hot steamy shower. I have tried to wash away everything that happened yesterday. Should I call this Adam person, or should I just get on with my life as if I was never exposed to the idea that there is someone else like me out there?

I trace the scars on my body from the time when I use to cut myself. They look ugly, but they remind me of a time that I never want to return to. I wonder if this Adam guy can help me figure out more about my powers.

I spend the day asking myself the normal question about the great dilemma of my life, *Should I please my father like normal children do, like this Nadeem boy, or should I just pursue my dreams?*

No matter how many times I ask myself this question, I am always scared that if I don't make it as a writer, my father will never take me back. But then, what if I do make it?

Again, maybe this Adam guy can help me figure myself out. I know it's wrong to pin all my hopes on one person, but he's the only other person who knows exactly what it's like to have this power. I sometimes wish I was as naïve as Nadeem and Karma, following their parent's footsteps because that's their reason for being here. But I am not naïve.

I get dressed and go to the 10am meeting anyway.

"You're late," Father tells me.

"It's 9:59am, I'm not late."

"You should have been here before this." He walks towards the conference room, gesturing at me to follow him.

Inside the conference room, Noah, Karma, and Jabril are waiting for us. As the meeting starts, I can't help drifting off into a world of my own. I'm thinking about the novel I dream of writing, thinking about the Master's I wish I could apply for. Thinking about how I feel like an outcast in this room full of business minds.

"So, Malikah, what do you think?" Jabril asks, smiling at me because he knows I wasn't listening, and he just wants to embarrass me. I think Karma got the essence of being an asshole from him.

"What?"

"This project, what do you think about it?"

I'm completely thrown, but I look at the papers in front of me, and the PowerPoint presentation on the screen. It's something about a new marketing strategy for AL-Hadidi real estate, our sister company.

"YeaH, it's perfect. Totally with it," I say, trying to look like I know what I am talking about.

"Oh God, she wasn't even listening. I don't even know what you are doing here," Karma says angrily. And now Father is looking at me with disapproval. He feels angry too. He feels that I am irresponsible, he feels like I'm going to mess up his legacy. Which is actually true; I am not a business-person. Anxiety kicks in as I start sweating, I have no idea what to say but then Noah swoops in to save the day.

"I think you are wrong, Karma, Malikah knows all about this project—we were just discussing it yesterday. Isn't it right, Malikah?"

"Yes, indeed, Noah."

And Noah goes on and on about a story that never happened, claiming I suggested some strategies which clearly are his own. He does all this just to save me from embarrassment. The meeting ends and as I leave the conference room, it feels like I can breathe again. Karma is burning with jealousy inside and it's not just the voices, it's in her eyes.

"Is everything alright?" Noah asks me. He is worried.

"It's nothing—I'm just thinking about my wasted youth."

Noah looks at me. His emotions are all over the place.

"Why did you even come today, Malikah?" he asks.

"I didn't have a choice, Noah."

"You do, you're just too scared to go after it, because there is a lot at stake. You know what, I am always worried about you, but you are not a child or a fucked-up teenager anymore, Malikah. If you don't want the life you are living, then get the fuck out of there and find the one that you *do* want. I am not going to save your ass every step of the way. What if one day I'm not there to help you? What would you do? You say women are oppressed by men yet you depend on me to save your ass!"

"I don't depend on you, you just save my ass. Don't do it if it's such a responsibility. I could've taken care of myself in there."

"Yes, right. Well, if you are so independent and know what you want, why don't you bravely go and fucking get it?"

I know he is right. I know every word he is saying is out of love for me, rather than anger. Noah has never spoken to me this way before. But I guess even he is fed up with the way I am living my life.

Chapter Fifteen

I am tossing clothes around. What on earth should I wear? Thankfully, my savior arrives just in time.

"Is it a date?" Sarah asks.

"What? NO!"

"Then why are you finding it so hard to pick an outfit?"

"Well, you have got to see this guy's eyes. Then you'd understand," I tell her, and can't help but smile.

She pouts at me and picks a simple outfit from my closet. A black skirt and a black velvet v-cut pullover. She takes out my half boots.

"Well, I've never seen you so curious and excited at the same time, so there," she says, laying the outfit on bed.

"Exactly what are you expecting to find out?" Her emotions are worried, as usual. She is scared I will be disappointed, and that maybe this guy doesn't hold all my answers. Honestly? I am scared too. Maybe he doesn't hold any of the answers but at least he'll understand what it's like to have this power.

"Noah told me what happened this morning," Sarah sighs. "I think he's right in some ways. But you're my best friend in the whole world. I get why you're acting so passive and why you are trying to please everyone." She comes closer and hugs me. "I believe in you, always." She hugs me tighter and I feel her love, her compassion, and her excessive caring for me and for everyone around her.

"I feel that maybe this person might be the answer," I finally confess. "Apart from his beautiful eyes, he has the same power. Maybe he knows why we are like this," I sigh. "And honestly, if he's not the answer, then at least I know I am not the only one."

"I understand. Just please be careful."
"I will," I promise.

I meet Adam in Cairo Cellar. We sit at the same table as before. The one where we met for the first time.

He automatically orders a jar of red wine sangria, just like the one I ordered yesterday.

I watch his eyes as he looks around and then back at me.

He has a black beard and short curly black hair. His looks are so innocent, yet I see pain and hints of a dreadful past in his eyes.

"What's your story?" I ask.

"My story?" he smiles. "I have so many, but sitting here, not hearing anything from your emotions is my favorite story so far. What's your story?"

"Short tempered."

"Oh, I'm sorry. Me too."

We look at each other for a moment. It's not a challenge, but it's not every day we meet someone we hear nothing from. There is no trust yet between us, but we are so used to knowing what people are feeling that *not knowing* is freaking us out.

"I'm sorry. I am just freaked out yesterday."

"Well, me too."

"Do you have any idea why we are like this?"

"Yes. I do," he sighs and takes a large sip from his glass. "Let me try to simplify it for you. Humans have something called a mirror neuron system. Normal empaths have hyper responsive mirror neurons, and because of this they are able to mirror other people's emotions and understand what they're feeling. For us super empaths, we aren't just hyper responsive. Our response takes a huge place in our mind, causing all our senses to know, feel, listen, and understand other people's emotions. There are also electromagnetic fields, which are generated by the brain and the heart and are responsible for transmitting information about people's thoughts and emotions. These fields are also extra sensitive for empaths, but for people like us, these fields spear out to all our senses. So, if normal empaths feel overwhelmed with emotions, we get totally fucked up." He takes a gulp from his glass, finishes it, and refills it again.

"You know basic science, the universe itself has magnetic fields and as they change, we are affected in so many ways. You'd have to ask a scientist about that; I am not a pro. What I understand is that empaths are more connected to the Earth than anyone else. And in our case, we *are* the Earth, we *are* emotions, basically, we *are* humanity. Normal human empaths can actually give others energy through their compassion, that's why emotions are contagious. In our case, we can heal others if we want to, through just one touch and a clear mind. Normal empaths can pair two different senses, but we can pair all five together without even trying. It's called synesthesia. Empaths feel other people's emotions like they are their own—this is called mirror-touch synesthesia. We feel other people's emotions and understand them like they are our own, but choosing to be affected by it or not—that is hard to control."

"How do you know all this?" I ask. I am awed, amazed, and overwhelmed by so much information.

"Well, mostly from books. And my aunt, who raised me, she is a psychologist. There is more… the amygdala in the brain is involved with the processing of emotions, memories, and motivation. It's an important part of something called the limbic system that is located above the brain stem and is highly involved with our emotions, our feelings of pleasure, and our memories. This part of our brains is extremely responsive and hyperactive. It also impacts on all parts of our senses and brain system. But this bit is too scientific for me and I don't really get it. I just know that we have fucking empathy superpowers." He takes a large sip. I am speechless and have no idea how I should respond.

"Did someone do experiments on you or something?" I ask eventually.

He looks at me and sighs. "Well, not exactly. My aunt wanted me to work with her in psychology, but I didn't want to be forced into it. And actually, I also wanted to be an athlete. I don't want to keep my powers from people—that would be selfish. But if I'm going to help, it has got to be in a way that I choose. It wasn't experiments precisely—it's just they have done so much work to try and understand how my brain functions. It's highly confidential work because no one knows we exist."

"What's wrong with helping other people with your powers?"

"Nothing. And I want to help others. But I can't do it if my mind is in pain or my emotions are fucked up. For us, we need to meditate and keep ourselves calm, or we won't be any good for anyone. I help her treat people with depression and that type of thing. It's my life's purpose, along with sports. But I also take time off once in a while so I can restore my energy."

"I understand."

"Well, I have helped lots of people. I still do."

"You come here to restore your energy?" I laugh. "This country is great, but Cairo is a city that never sleeps."

"I grew up here," he tells me, and his expression changes. I immediately know there is a story behind that statement.

"If you don't mind telling me, why do you feel like it's your life's purpose to heal others?"

He doesn't answer immediately. He just takes another sip and refills his glass.

"Well, I guess I don't want to be the person who has the power to do something good, but who chooses not to use it. I am a good guy."

"There is more, I know I might not hear your emotions, but your eyes are telling me that there is more."

"Let's just say that I don't know you well enough to tell you yet. Now it's your turn to talk. What's your story, Malikah?" He says my name slowly, spelling each letter as if his life depends on it. I have never realized how beautiful my name is.

"Well, Adam." I say his name the same way, hoping he feels something because I can't be the only one here.

"I am the daughter of one of the most arrogant, powerful, and self-centered rich men in the middle east," I laugh. "God, people think I care but I really don't, he has never made any effort to get to know me, and my mother left when I was twelve years old. She ran away to London and never came back. I missed her at first, but then I got used to being alone," I say, trying to sound casual but knowing it's killing me from the inside. All these flashbacks at once. *Keep calm, Malikah.*

"Well, I live with my aunt. Actually she's not my aunt, she's my mother's best friend. My mother died when I was twelve years old, leaving me with an abusive father. That's why Lina took me away. Ironically enough, to London." He smiles, "We all suffer. I am not underestimating your past experiences or your life. I can just tell that you have really suffered, and I want you to know that we all do. Me and you suffer in a completely different way for sure." He smiles and puts his hands on mine. I can feel my whole body tremble, I can feel the warmth of his hands on my dead cold body. He takes his hands off after few seconds.

"I don't hear your emotions, but I have to know that I am not the only one feeling this?" he asks, and I can see worry in his eyes. It feels like there is this inexplicable magnet between us, getting stronger all the time. Maybe it's because we feel so calm sitting here together, with no emotions to listen to, and time stands still for a moment.

Then my phone pings, and the moment is cut short.

"That's weird," I say, looking at the screen.

"What?"

"It's my mother." I take a deep breath, "She's coming to Cairo and wants to meet me." I laugh. "That's funny, it has been ten years, why would she want to meet me now?"

He looks at me and says, "Well, then you've got to meet her. She is your mother."

"We might be feeling some kind of connection here, but please don't talk about my mother."

"Alright, I'm sorry."

I smile at his immediate apology. He didn't have to say sorry, but he did anyway.

"What time is it?" I ask.

"8pm."

"Wow, we've been here two hours, can I take you someplace else?"

"Yeah sure! Where to?"

"Just trust me," I say, smiling.

Chapter Sixteen

It's a beautiful evening. I take him to the place I go to when I want to remember who I am. When I want to escape all my crowded thoughts, emotions, and worries. We reach the Art Café in el Zamalek. It's open mic day.

"I am not Malikah here, I am the poet."

"What?" he laughs.

"Just go along with it. No one here knows my name, they just call me the poet. You can check my Instagram. Zero photos, only poems."

"Oh, okay I'll play along."

We enter the café and everyone greets me. I sit Adam on the first table in front of the stage. Ten minutes pass and the MC introduces me to the stage. Everyone applauds, they know me and I can see the surprise in Adam's eyes.

"Hello, everyone. Today, I'm going to read a poem I've just finished called Life as An Empath."

I adjust the mic and take a deep breath. I try not to let my anxiety take over. Every time I am on that stage I try to shift from Malikah the passive, the pleaser, the one who's forced into a life she has no choice in, into Malikah, the poet, the writer, the lover. The real Malikah I strive to be.

"Oh, dear God, you gave me powers to feel so much, yet speak so little.

Oh, dear God, you gave me powers to see through and beyond skin, bones, and colors.

I wonder if it's a blessing, or a curse.

I wonder if it's goodness or is it darkness dressed as brave?

I am not brave, because I fear so much.

I fear I am not enough.

I fear helplessness.
Sometimes I fear that I am being too tough.
So, am I? Am I brave? Am I brave to feel or will it be the end of my years?

"Oh, dear God as I pray,
I wish for peace, light, and love to stay.
I know peace is momentary.
I know darkness is obligatory.
But love will keep me here…
Love will lift me up, save me, and embrace my fears.
An empath who feels.
An empath who writes poetry with tears.
An empath who wants to give so much
Yet feels so empty and so drained.
But still, an empath never gives up.
God has blessed me with so much,
A heart that feels, gives and loves,
A mind that thinks and opens up.
In the end I am just a human, half angel, half demon.
This is who I am, an angelic empath with a devilish soul.

I guess I have learned throughout the years
To love my darkness more.
I saw my light so late in years,
I saw it late I didn't know it was there.
Until I found and spread my wings so wide I'm free.
God, I know life is not fair.
My light and darkness are not even on the same scale.
I know, I know, I know, I understand.
The load is too much for a human soul,
But an empath is a superhuman.
Who feels so deep and loves too much.

I guess it's a blessing sometimes,
Other times it is a curse controlling my mind.
Oh, dear God give me strength,
To love, not to hate and to always give.

Oh, dear God I'd rather be poor than rich,
If rich is where humanity fades
Then I'd rather be a poor human.
I'd rather wear silver if diamonds build egos
I'd rather live in a cottage in the forest.
If houses build jealousy.

I want to be human.
I want to remain an empath.
I want to write my heart out,
My pain, my loneliness, and my suffering.
I want to be a human filled with humanity,
Not a human robot filled with greed and insensibility.
It's a blessing, it's a blessing.
It's a curse, a wonderful curse.
I am poetic even in pain.
But that's what an empath does.
I promise It's not in vain…"

The crowd applauds and screams, "Hail the Poet!" and I see Adam in the front row smiling so hard I am sure his face hurts. He looks at me with his beautiful eyes, they light up like a movie actor's. He stands and claps and whispers, *I love it*. Making sure that I can read his lips as he does so. I motion for the back-stage team to start the music. I start singing "One More Light" by Linkin Park. Every time I sing a song by them, my eyes tear up. This is where I belong. Poetry, music. And Emotions. That's where I belong.

I sing my heart out. I always feel scared as I step on the stage. But then when I start reciting my poetry, or singing my choice of song, I feel free. I feel like anything is possible. Like my worries are nothing and that my dreams are everything. I finish the song and bow to the small audience that in my heart feels so big because for me this is where I let out the real version of me, Malikah the poet.

"I'm amazed, but confused. I didn't know you write."

"Well, I thought I'd tell you in a creative way," I smile and sit down next to him. "This is my secret identity, it's the only place I feel like myself," I tell him.

"Why is it a secret?" he asks. "This has to come out to the whole world."

"Well, my father isn't one to accept this version of me."

"So?" he asks as if this is a weird and unconvincing reason. "Are you going to live in his shadow? I might not know you very well yet, Malikah, but I am going to. So far you have amazed me and surprised me and made me feel things I never thought I'd feel." He takes my hand and says, "I practice parkour and extreme sports, you know how many people think I am crazy? Even my aunt. But they have no choice. It's my life to live. I go out there and do the one thing I love, the one thing I am passionate about. It's a waste of time if you don't pursue what you want in life. Life is meaningless without passion, and even more meaningless when you have passion and do nothing about it."

"Well, I get that but…"

He interrupts my words, "No buts. Just let my words sink in. You're brave enough to do anything, anyway."

We look at each other and I get lost in his eyes. We laugh and we talk and it feels so familiar, even though we don't know each other that well yet.

We go back to his two-bedroom apartment with its high ceiling in Zamalek. He makes me a hot chocolate with marshmallows on top. He tells me that he and his aunt live in this apartment, but that she rarely comes to Egypt. He comes about once every three months or so. We sit on the couch in his living room. The house is simple, with warm colors and a cozy, homey feeling. It has a soul, unlike the penthouse I live in.

We sit there looking into each other's eyes, enjoying the silence, the calmness, and the mutual understanding of just wanting to sit in calmness together. He leans forward and I don't move.

He caresses my face, then my lips. I can feel his breath so close to my face. I lean in close enough to kiss, but I don't.

He leans in more and kisses my lips with his soft, full mouth. It is a soft, passionate, and deep kiss. I can smell his scent, feel his touch, listen to his heart, and taste his tongue. I see his emotions in every movement. And I know in this moment, we feel exactly the same.

He leans backwards and I say, "You taste like chocolate."

"Hmm, and you smell like roses," he smiles.

"Was this a date?" I ask.

"It took me so much time to get dressed, so I guess it's a date. But I'd rather take you out on a real date if you don't mind. This wasn't supposed to be one. It just turned out that way."

I smile at him. "Well, we'll have to schedule a real date then."

"Indeed, we will."

We kiss some more and the alarm on my phone rings.

"Oh shit, I have to go. It's my curfew."

"Curfew? You're 21!"

"Yeah, but I have a middle eastern father. We're in Egypt. I am a woman. So, I have a curfew unfortunately," I say sarcastically.

"When will I see you again?" he asks, and he looks like a little baby who has lost his mother in in the grocery store.

I kiss him one more time. "When you ask me out on a real date."

"Okay, I'll ask you out on a date tomorrow. Maybe I'll bring flowers."

"Make sure they're red roses then," I smile.

"Okay, ma'am!" he says, smiling as I close the door behind me.

I feel my heart pounding—partly because of all the day's emotions, but also because I am so late.

"Totally worth it," I tell myself.

I am back home that night just before the clock strikes twelve. I feel like Cinderella, and not just because of the curfew.

I find Sarah in my room reading. I smile at her, and she knows immediately.

"So, it *was* a date!" I hear her happy emotions. It has been so long since I felt anything good. "Tell me all about it. I am staying the night because of this Adam boy so you're not going to sleep until you tell me what happened," she says.

We hear a knock on the door and Father comes in. I sit up, the smile fading from my face.

"Meeting tomorrow at 11:00 am, make sure you're not late to this one," he tells me.

I try not to feel drained; I remember what Adam told me, and what Noah shouted in my face.

"Are you going?" Sarah asks.

I look at her and break a smile, "I don't know."

Chapter Seventeen

I arrive at the office at 10am sharp. Father is surprised. I am wearing his favorite suit. He likes it when I wear the things he buys. I fake a smile all day, because this is the version of me that he likes. I don't even know what I'm doing anymore. I don't know why I came, but I just did. Still the pleaser inside of me won't subside.

During the meeting, I'm extremely attentive and responsive. Business school taught me a thing or two even though I literally cheated my way out of it just to be able to pass. Noah is eyeing me in disagreement, and I know now that I have disappointed him by coming to the office again. He wanted me to sit on my ass and start my story. If I'm honest, I am disappointed in me too. On the other hand, Karma is eyeing me with hatred because now I am so responsive, and I've come up with some really creative ideas that are stepping on her territory.

God, no one likes me in this room. Jabril is looking at me with amazement, but also a little bit of hatred because why in hell does he have to listen to a twenty-one-year-old talking about the future of business? The only proud person in the room is Father. Of course, he doesn't show it. He would burn before he shows any sign of satisfaction or feeling proud. Me, amongst all of the emotions I am listening to now, I don't feel proud or satisfied or annoyed or angry. I feel misplaced. Like a puzzle piece being forced into the wrong place, or a wolf trying to blend in among lions. I am the color black in a rainbow; I will never fit in. I think about that a lot, but actually, do I even want to fit in?

We finish the meeting and I head back to my office. Finally alone for a moment, I shake off all the emotions I've been overwhelmed by all day. I can't get Adam out of my mind and I can't wait for our date tonight. I hear the door open. Its Karma and she's full of anger.

"Are you trying to raise my blood pressure or something? Seriously what the hell are you doing here?"

I look at her, and I try to sound in control, like I know what I'm doing. But actually, I don't.

"Existing," I answer.

"Well, go exist someplace else! This place is clearly not for you. You think you can do it all, don't you? I have worked my ass off. I am one of the youngest people to actually create something in this business. Go do something you're actually good at. Because you can't pull this off, Queen Malikah," she says and leaves the room.

She is right.

Father comes into my office. Although at least he knocked this time. "We have dinner tonight with Nadeem and Mr. Maged."

"What? No, I have plans," I say immediately.

"Cancel them."

"I can't."

He looks at me and it feels like he could burn me with his look.

"I said, cancel them," he tells me slowly, spelling out each letter. I remember the way Adam said my name and I realize how completely different my two worlds are.

I call Adam and tell him about the emergency meeting. He sounds disappointed and asks me to cancel it, but I carefully explain why I can't.

"I wish you would live like Malikah, not his Malikah," he responds. And it shocks me.

"You know he has the power to destroy my life, Adam."

"Oh, really? How? By taking your money?"

"That's the least he would do."

"Well, if that's what you are afraid of, if that's what is stopping you from actually finding yourself and discovering the world your own way, if that's what is convincing you that being a pleaser is better than embracing who you are, then fine. Convince yourself all you want, Malikah. I thought your passion is much stronger than this."

"Good, but Adam, I'll see you soon." I hang up, trying to ignore what he just said. I always say that people don't like the raw and blunt truth because it's hard to face your reality. In this moment I understand how true this is.

I go to my father's dinner anyway. I sit there in silence while they talk about business. Nadeem watches me, wishing he could open a conversation.

"Why are you here?" he smiles "I thought it's just me who is my father's puppet."

"Excuse me, Mr. Maged, I am never going to marry your son," I announce.

"Excuse me?" Mr. Maged splutters, looking at me and then back at my father.

"Well, sir, your son is such a daddy's boy, and I have always despised being my father's puppet. I'm not going to marry a puppet," I smile and look at Nadeem. "Now, Nadeem, you are the only daddy's puppet on this table. Goodbye."

I glare at them all with anger and feel victorious. Without hesitation, I stand up and say, "I have got to go now."

I leave without waiting for any response, without waiting for Father's orders. I know he will fuck me up later. But I am done being trapped. I am done being a prisoner. I am done obeying and listening to a world, a father, a society that wants me to be everything and anything other than myself. I have never felt more powerful. I have never felt so myself. I think about all the times that I have obeyed everyone and everything around me, trying so hard to be what everyone wanted and needed. Tried to please Father and society by being someone I am not.

I embrace myself with everything that I am. I might not know where to go from here or what I am going to do, but I know that starting now, I'm only going to be myself.

I go to Adam's apartment and knock on the door.

"Malikah."

"You are completely right. I should live how Malikah wants."

I throw myself at him and we kiss passionately and deeply. I have never felt such a profound emotion of my own. I have never felt so free. He makes me feel free; like I can be whoever I want.

"I want to know more! I want to know if there is more to life, if there is more to these empathy powers," I sigh. "I want a way out of all of this, and I believe that meeting you is the sign I needed. I can't tolerate being the passive pleaser I have always been. No more."

My father keeps calling me, but I don't answer. When I finally give in and pick up the phone, he is screaming as if I am the world's worst human.

"It's going to be okay," Adam tells me. But he has no idea. Nothing is going to be okay.

We lie on his bed, cuddling for a while. I don't want to leave. I want to never leave. But I have to, eventually.

I get back home before Father does.

I change into my pajamas and I wait for a fight.

He slams the door open.

"What the hell did you do? You embarrassed me in front of my friend and his son. Do you even have a fucking brain, Malikah?"

"I didn't want to sit there. I told you I had plans. I told you I didn't want to go but YOU NEVER LISTEN," I shout with all my heart.

"Oh, I never listen, huh? You are such an irresponsible, ungrateful, and completely unreliable child. I should have thrown you away when you were born, or given you to your crazy, fucked up mother."

My heart is pounding, but not with fear. It is pounding with anger. I feel anger soaking me. His anger and mine.

"Anything would've been way better than living with a disrespectful, womanizing, arrogant man who never listens or tries to actually get to know his daughter." This has come from the deepest, darkest corners of my heart.

And for the first time, my father raises his hand and slaps me so hard that I fall down on the floor.

"You don't deserve anything I do," he says. "You're wasting your life on trivial things, wanting to be God knows what. I am trying to give you position, power, and everything you please."

My tears are pouring down my face, I look up at him with one hand on my right cheek.

"Well, not all people want what you want," I tell him. "There are things money can't buy—like a father who listens and understands, like a caring mother and like a fucking normal mind."

I scream my heart out and I don't even try to stop my tears. I stand up and take my hand away from my cheek so that he can see what he has done.

"I will NEVER be who you want me to be. I'd rather die than be your puppet. You think it's fine, hitting me, because we live in a patriarchal society. Well, that's not going to make me your puppet either, dear Father," I laugh and now he is even more angry and irritated. But I have never felt so much like myself before. "You think this luxurious house and these branded clothes and expensive watches make you a better person, but it doesn't. Money doesn't determine your value, or how good or unique a person you are. Money doesn't determine shit, Father. You hide behind this persona, but you are as cheap as fuck. You have no humanity and no empathy towards the people around you. You think you can buy anything or be anything because you have power, well you can't be a good father, or a decent husband. You think I want your money? I just wanted you to be there. I wanted you to listen. Do you know what I want to do in my life? Do you even know what I am passionate about? You just want to shape me like a Barbie doll, dress me and brush my hair and make me into a female version of yourself. But unfortunately, Father, I am too much of a human, too much of emotions, too much of an empath to be this fucked up version you are trying to create. So, go on, hit me again. It reminds me more of who I want to be. The pain I feel is nothing compared to the agony, rage, and the feeling of being an outcast that I have felt every day of my life."

He looks at me in disgust, and disappointment. He slaps me again, hard.

"Let's see which will be more painful then."

I look at him in disbelief, but I don't stop crying; this time I won't. I am going to cry my heart out. I'm going to let it all out. He leaves the room and slams the door.

I have hurt his pride and his precious manhood. I have hurt what's left of his emotions and I have pounded all his patriarchal ideologies into dirt by standing up after falling down.

But I don't care now, because I am not going to hide who I am anymore.

Chapter Eighteen

Telling Noah what I've done was like throwing him a surprise party. Sarah, on the other hand, was just waiting for it to happen, so she didn't seem so surprised. However, they both shared the same emotions. They were proud that I actually stood up for myself. That I said exactly how I felt. I can't say it turned out the way I wanted, but at least I know now that I won't let my emotions subside, or keep them at bay anymore.

For a whole month I've tried to avoid my father in every way possible, except when Noah forces me to go to the family dinner. Father definitely feels that I am the one in the wrong, for being such a rude and irresponsible person. Well, good luck with that, because I am not going to apologize either. He's been avoiding me as well. I know it's because he has been shocked by what I said, but he won't admit it. So instead he chooses to be the one who's upset about all of this, the one waiting for me to apologize. I think the big blue bruises on my cheeks are enough proof of who exactly is the wrong one.

At the dining table, Father keeps talking about what I did. Jabril and Karma's response is to blindly accept what he says. They even seem convinced that he was right to slap my face. Noah disagrees with all his heart, because hitting a woman is no option, and it would've been easier to just actually listen.

"You two are in your own little gang, aren't you?" Father asks him.

"No, Uncle Zayne, that's not it. I know Malikah, she is so much more than what you all see."

I sit still and try to ignore the fact that they are talking about me as if I am not even there. But then the weirdest thing happens. Uncle Bilal speaks out.

"Well, I think Malikah has got more to say than anyone else at this table, and if she wants to be a writer then we'd be such a bad family if we didn't support her. I think hitting a woman is savage; we're not in the ages of slavery. I know this society is still very patriarchal but, god damn it, we are in 2021. Do you think your daughter will marry someone you choose, or grow up to be exactly as you want? That would mean she has no individual, independent personality. Whereas obviously she is stunningly creative," Uncle Bilal says, looking at me. "Be what you want to be, do what you want to do, love and marry who you want to love, write and create the art you please. No one here is you and no one ever will be. Embrace that."

He finishes his sentence, and everyone looks at him in surprise. Usually Bilal doesn't get involved in any of our conversations, he doesn't talk much or react much. He has his own business, his own life. In fact, no one really knows what he does. And for the first time in years I have heard him engaged, and all because of me! His emotions are very precise, they are so wise and loving. They are of justice and truth. He is like a saint but with a very terrible past. He chooses to talk only when necessary. I look back at him with my eyes full of tears. I know he felt this was an important thing to say. He continues his meal as if he hasn't spoken. But even though his emotions are so precise, he is also, for some reason, extremely nervous. I guess it's because we never really talked to each other that much, and now here he is standing up for me. He has said the words I wished to be said.

I want to scream YES, but I keep quiet. I don't want to gloat. The youngest of my father's brothers is the wisest of them all. He is the one who saw through my situation, instead of just repeating the hurting words that have been said to me all day.

Bilal looks at me again and smiles. It feels like he is forcing this smile because he doesn't seem to know how to smile. But I smile back anyway, because he understands me. He has realized that Father has been mocking me, and making fun of me, to prove me wrong in front of the whole family.

Bilal actually listened to the meaning between the words. I think he understands the meaning of my words because he has been there and being misjudged, misunderstood, and mistreated is familiar to him. I am sure they made fun of him when he decided to stop being a CEO in a multi-million dollar company and instead created an interior design company. I bet they laughed as he pursued his art—making furniture and decorating homes to make them beautiful. I have never felt that curious towards Uncle Bilal. His emotions are usually very calm, and sarcastic deep down. Today, his emotions are very precise and very clear. Father seems displeased. I don't know if it's because Uncle Bilal is on my side, or if it's because he spoke at all. Suddenly Father's emotions become jealous and his anger rises.

"Well, Bilal, my daughter is nothing like you. She will never be. I'm glad you found your path away from the family business; you weren't very good at it anyway. Malikah on the other hand is a genius."

"Genius?" Karma spits, laughing loudly. "Uncle Zayne, she clearly hates what we do. I say let's put her out of her misery." Her eyes light up at the idea.

Father looks at her in disagreement, getting angrier by the second. "You better behave. Malikah is your next CEO. Now we shall end this discussion."

Chapter Nineteen

I cry myself to sleep each night, although I'm trying to break this habit. It has been years since I really cried my heart out. Normally, I keep it all in. But if I am embracing myself and my powers then I better let some emotions out. On Friday night, I sneak out to meet Adam, when Father and Tina have left for a party at their friend's house.

I've sneaked out every day—it wasn't a new thing—but today was different.

"Wow, your uncle seems cool!" Adam tells me, stroking my hair.

I love sleeping on his chest and hearing his heartbeat. It makes me feel safe and calm.

"Yeah, I know! I never really knew him, you know. He left the company years ago and created his own interior design company. I think he pursued what he loved. I love and respect that about him. But my father's emotions were burning up when Bilal talked. It's like there was some kind of unfinished business between them. I guess it's because Bilal is successful on his own. Father must hate that."

We pause for a moment and look into each other's eyes, but then Adam's phone rings. He looks at it and quickly stands up.

"I have to take this, love, just a moment," he says and hurries into his bedroom. I sit on the couch and wait for him, but I can't help wonder why he didn't take the call in front of me. I try to ignore my trust issues and the fact that I am incapable of listening to his emotions and instead try to appreciate his existence—because he is the only other person on Earth like me.

He returns to the room as he finishes the call. "Sorry, love, it was my aunt."

"It's okay," I smile at him. "Everything alright?"

"Yes, don't worry. She was just checking. So, tell me, did your mother call you again?"

"She keeps calling me, but I don't answer her that much. And she hasn't told me when she's coming."

"May I ask why you don't pick up?"

"Well, because she left me—why would I care?"

"Is there some other reason?"

I look at him and feel my heart pounding. There is another reason, but I don't want to talk about it.

"It's okay, we don't have to talk about it now."

"Yes please."

"I love you."

"What?" I look at him in amazement. "You love me?"

"Yes, actually. I know it's too early to say it, and I know you are probably freaking out right now, but I have been feeling it for a while. Damn it, I have felt it since the day I met you. I wanted you to know that I love you, because I am scared."

I stand up and move closer to him. "Why are you scared?"

"Well, I have never loved anyone before. It's a pretty weird feeling, and its overwhelming. The emotions I have for you are endless. But I don't want to freak you out."

"Oh God. I love you too, Adam."

"You do?"

"Yes, of course. I mean I still have my doubts but that's because I have been through so much. You appeared in the weirdest, yet truest phase in my life. How can I not love you? You are like god sent or something."

He smiles and it is the most childlike smile, pure and innocent as if I've given him the world in the palm of his hand. I am only one person. I am not the world but I do love him so much. I am scared too but it's worth it because nothing ever feels like this. It's an ineffable emotion that I have never truly felt before. This is the love I have been waiting for. The love that lights up my soul.

He embraces me and whispers, "I love you. I want to say it all the time."

I giggle and kiss him. I kiss him with everything in me. I kiss him with passion, love, understanding, and connection. I kiss him but it isn't just a kiss, it is a promise that this love is unique and adventurous. A promise that this love will last for life.

"I love you, Adam," I whisper.

Chapter Twenty

I left the house that day angry and crying over my father's words but came home feeling loved and appreciated. It's a strange world. You feel like days look alike but they are not. And before you notice, a year can pass and things can change, and you have no control over anything at all. I started writing my novel the day Father slapped me on the face. I think I needed to let out my emotions and I ended up writing the brief description of the novel I want to write. It's basically the story of a lady trying to figure out herself among different choices and paths. It's me in another character. I think all writers leave a piece of themselves in their writings and for me it's all I am doing now.

I don't know where I'll go with this novel, I just know that I will keep writing it and outlining everything until I figure it out.

I try to sneak into the house, but the door won't open. There is a leg on the floor, blocking the doorway. I push the door harder and the leg moves enough for me to slide through the door. I find Uncle Bilal lying on the floor behind the door.

"Uncle Bilal, what are you doing sleeping on the floor?"

He doesn't answer. He smells like a bottle of black label whisky. He must have been drinking too much.

I put my hand on his shoulders and push him softly to wake him up.

"Oh Malikah, sorry, honey. I think I fell over!" he laughs.

"What are you doing here?"

"Well, me and your father were having a talk and when he left I started drinking alone but I think I finished the bottle." He smiles but his eyes are shut. I have to move him but he is very heavy.

His black hair is messed up. His brown eyes are red now and his emotions are all over the place.

"Come on, let me help you." I put his hands on my shoulders and hug him so that I can lift him up. "Let's get up on the count of three, okay?"

"Oh-kay," he says, and he leans his head to the side. I count but he doesn't help me get him up.

I call Noah for back up, and he appears from downstairs, wearing his pajamas.

"Wow, he is hammered," Noah laughs.

"Less talking, more lifting."

Noah and I lift Uncle Bilal up and try to wake him up enough so that he can walk to the guest room.

"What is he doing here? Isn't his apartment downstairs?"

"Yeah, but apparently he and my father were talking and he ended up drinking the whole bottle alone."

We put him down in the guest room and I take off his shoes. He looks at us and says, "Thank you, guys, you are the best. Nothing like your fathers." And gives us the thumps up.

Me and Noah look at each other and frown.

"What do his emotions tell you?"

"Broken, fragile, lost, and vulnerable. I think his heart is broken. His emotions are fragile and that makes him vulnerable. And because he is heart-broken, he feels lost. I knew he was emotional."

"He doesn't seem like it. But I guess you would know, my Super Lady!" Noah says, smiling. "I have to go now because I have a meeting tomorrow, let's meet tomorrow and talk okay?"

"Okay, I'll stay with him for a while."

Noah leaves me alone with Uncle Bilal. He tries, and fails, to sit up.

"You can sleep, you know."

"Yes, but I want to tell you a story," he says, without even opening his eyes. "But first, you have got to stop calling me Uncle Bilal, how old am I? 50?" he laughs at his own joke. I laugh too, reassured that he wants to be my friend.

"Well, Bilal," I say, smiling. "Tell me a story then."

"Oh, you are a listener, aren't you? You are nothing like your father." He laughs again but this time I frown. He opens his eyes. "I'm sorry. I can't sleep when I am too drunk. I wait for sleep to invade me instead."

"Yeah, I understand."

"Okay, so the story is about the woman who stole my heart," he smiles. "She had beautiful blonde curly hair and a stunning smile that could light up the whole room. I painted her in many of my canvases." He puts a finger to his lips. "But don't tell anybody," he whispers.

"I won't, Bilal, I promise."

"We were in an impossible relationship. It broke my heart to lose her."

"Why did you have to lose her?"

"Because I had to." His eyes suddenly water up and tears come streaming down his face. "I have been filling the void with so many things, but I know I will never love anyone the way I loved her."

"And where is she now?"

"Gone," he sighs.

His emotions are a mess. When he started talking about this woman, his emotions started to light up and scream, consuming him, his heart, and his mind, poor Bilal. It made me think about Adam and how much I love him. Heartbreak is the worst when love is as true as this. Heartbreak is even worse when it has consumed you and made you feel lost for years. Bilal never got over this woman, but she didn't break his heart. She just left.

"I know you are not a happy person, but it's okay, it's going to be alright. Believe in that. Find something that inspires you and do it, Malikah. It will be the best thing you'll ever do, trust me. Passion is a beautiful thing and when it's done with all that you are, it'll make this life worth living." He pauses and then takes a deep breath, "I left the family business and started my own years ago. You know what I did?"

"What?"

"I painted murals and did more freelance work on the side, while taking courses in interior design. I was a business major—I knew nothing about interior design, but I love to paint." He smiles and I can hear his passion. "I disappointed the whole family," he continues. "But I was so proud of myself for doing what I love. Painting and creating fuels the fires of passion inside my soul. Does that make sense?" he asks.

I smile at him. "It makes perfect sense."

He closes his eyes and finally falls asleep. I don't know if he'll remember our conversation, but I am glad it happened. He was vulnerable and honest. His barriers were down, and his emotions were scattered all over. Artists are like that. I think we build barriers because we are too emotional and too vulnerable. It makes us feel weak and different, but when those barriers are down, there is a whole other person in there. A whole other world with a different kind of beauty. The beauty of vulnerability, honesty, love, passion, and emotions. Artist or no artist; any person who is emotional or empathetic will know what I mean. For the very first time, I don't feel like such a misfit in the family, because now I know Bilal is as much a misfit as I am.

Chapter Twenty-One

I wake up to the sound of a phone ringing. It has been two months since my father and I spoke. My mother keeps calling me every once in a while, but she hasn't yet come to Cairo.

This time though, it's not my mother burning the phone, waking me up from a good sleep, it's Sarah. Her mother is back in the hospital. I hear her say she's in intensive care, but I can't understand anything else. I dress as quickly as possible, and then I notice a missed call from my mother.

I'll call her later, I tell myself. As I'm leaving, my father shouts at me.

"Did you know your mother is coming to Cairo?" he asks with rage in his eyes.

"Yes," I say bluntly. "I really have to go."

"Wait here, young lady. Do not turn your back on me when I am talking to you."

I take a deep breath and look at him. "Yes?"

"Are you planning to see her?" he asks and now I can sense his fear.

"Why do you care? She is my mother and I can see her if I want."

"Oh really? The mother who left you behind? You know I forbid you from seeing her years ago."

"Well, times have changed."

He stands up and approaches me, but I can still sense his fear. Why is he so concerned if I see her or not? It has been years. God, doesn't this man ever grow up?

"What, are you going to slap me again?"

"No. But if I ever see you anywhere near her, Malikah, you will regret it for the rest of your life," he says confidently. But I hear his fear.

"Why are you afraid?" I ask, looking deeply into his eyes. I see through him. "I mean you say it with confidence, but it seems like you are afraid."

He takes a step backwards and looks at me. "Afraid?" he asks with a fake laugh. Anyone else would believe that laugh. But I know he is faking. I am listening now. I don't ignore my emotions anymore. He is probably screaming in his head now, *How did she know I was afraid?* but I kind of like freaking people out like that.

"Laugh all you want. There is something that is making you terrified. Maybe if I see my mother I will just run away and leave you for good."

"Oh, dear, you are incapable of that. I can bring you home, no matter where you are."

"Yeah, I am sure. All hail King Zayne. Goodbye. My real family needs me now."

I walk away and hear his emotions rise. I hear his anger and his fear. He isn't going to hit me again, but he feels like he wants to. He is afraid of something, but I don't know what it is. Did my mother call him? I have no idea, but this makes me want to see her more than anything now.

I rush to the hospital and hover outside Sarah's mum's room. I can see Sarah sitting on a chair, holding her mother's hand. Sarah doesn't wear her hair in a ponytail, ever—she likes it loose and free, just like her soul. But today she has it up in a messy ponytail, and she is sleeping.

"She got out of intensive care a few minutes ago," Noah says. I hear his fear and his worry about Sarah and her mother.

"Do you think she'll make it this time? She has been so sick this past year."

He sighs and says, "I wish, Malikah, I really wish. I was kind of hoping to ask Sarah to marry me soon."

I look at him and smile, "What!? You're kidding me."

"No," he smiles back. "I mean it's about time, right? We've been together, what, two years? And we have been friends for seven or more years, thanks to you. I am so ready for this."

"Isn't she going to London for the scholarship?"

"What makes you think I'll let her go alone? I'm gonna be there, cheering for her to be the best psychologist there is."

"Oh God, I don't know how to feel now. I am so happy for you, but so worried about Amal."

"Well, let's just hope things go well."

I see Amal wake up and I quietly enter her room, gently waking Sarah up.

"Oh, you came." Sarah stands up and hugs me tightly. She feels like she is in pain, not just one pain but mental, emotional, and physical pain. Her mother is all she has. Her father died from depression years ago. That's why Sarah has chosen to specialize in psychology—she hopes she can help people get over their depression and their worries, so that no one dies of sadness ever again. She may have no superpowers like me, but she is so much more a superhero than I will ever be.

"Oh, Auntie Amal, are you feeling better?"

"They always say it's a coma. I say it's just a little bit of high blood pressure. Damn doctors don't know shit," Amal says, and I laugh my heart out. She is lying there with all these wires around her, and she still finds fun in being sick. She hates doctors so much; she doesn't tolerate hospitals.

"Oh, you're gonna be okay."

"Of course, dear. I am a fighter. And also, I want out of this hell hole."

"Mom, you're not going anywhere until you're better."

"This baby girl always worries." Amal looks at me and points at Sarah.

Sarah rolls her eyes and says, "Well, you're all I have. Plus, I have good news."

"Finally," Amal says.

"I got the scholarship and I am taking you with me."

Amal's eyes are so full of pride for her only daughter. "Oh, I always knew that you're a dreamer like your father, but unlike him, you actually break down the barriers and pursue your dreams. I am so proud of you." There are tears pouring pour down her face. Sarah leans in and hugs her, kissing her forehead.

"Oh, don't start crying, you know I'll cry too," Sarah says, but I know they are tears of happiness, love, and family. Something I have never experienced. I stand there watching them share this intimate moment of pride and joy. I hear Amal's emotions of pride and happiness. She could almost get up and run with the amount of joy she is feeling now. Sarah's emotions are worried but happy, because she has made her mother happy and her mother has always encouraged her to follow her dreams. Sarah's father worked in the stock market. He was the type of man who admired luxury and power, as many men do. In his case it led him to a long slow death—he lost too much money on the stock market and became depressed. They had to sell their big house and settle in a normal size apartment. Sarah didn't mind then because he was home more often but no one knew how depressed he was. Sarah grew to understand this as the years went by and her mother became the provider. But then one day they found him dead, sitting in his usual chair. He had lost everything, and left them with nothing. Sarah was 15 years old but she was smart enough to know that her father wasn't crazy; he was depressed. He died of sadness.

Sarah then decided that she wouldn't end up this way. Her mother raised her well, to be lose and free and hopeful. This is why she never wears her hair in a ponytail. I look at them, and I know that I will never have this. I don't have a mother who will be there at every step, or a father whose sole priority is his family.

I go outside, back to Noah. I can't help my thoughts, but if there is anything I hate, its jealousy. I am not jealous of Sarah, I am just sad that I never had this bond.

"It's okay, you know," Noah says.

"What is?"

"Well, you miss your mother. Admit it."

"No. I have no mother."

"Well, you know what I mean."

Noah looks at me and I feel his caring and his love. It's a blessing that makes me feel a little bit hopeful.

"She called me, you know. She is coming to Cairo."

"Then why the hell didn't you tell me? We should go see her."

"I don't know when she'll be here," I say and then I tell him about the weird conversation between me and Father this morning.

"But, Malikah, he has forbidden you from seeing her since the day she left. Don't you remember?"

"I do. I know," I pause. "I just don't believe anything he says now. Before I just did what he asked me to, because I thought that was the right thing to do. But him forbidding me from seeing my mother was one of the worst things I've ever had to endure. I don't know her though, Noah. I don't even know what to say to her."

"Well, you don't have to know anything. Just do it."

Sarah comes out to join us and we share a group hug. "I am so glad you guys are here. I know it's hard for you to be here, Malikah. I know how much you hate hospitals."

"Yeah, but it's your mother—the only mother figure I know," I smile. "You didn't tell me you got the scholarship?"

"You got the scholarship?" Noah asks in amazement. "Oh my God, we should celebrate!"

"I was going to tell you today, but then Mom got sick and… you know the rest."

Noah hugs Sarah. "Oh God, I am so proud of you. You worked so hard for it."

"You're squeezing me." Sarah starts to laugh.

He lets her go and we all laugh.

"I know I worked hard, it's my passion, guys. I am going to work for it all the way. I really want to be a research psychologist. I know I am a geek, but this is what I love. When something is done with passion it's done right, because no matter the obstacles and the hardships you face, you will do your best to overcome it all. Because you know deep down that you'll get to go where your passion leads you."

Noah and I look at her with awe and love. Sarah is in a different situation from us, but she never gave up on what she wants. This makes me overthink every hopeless detail of my life. When you do something with passion, it's done with love and a determination to get what you want; to be the person you strive to be, and to be the best version of who you are.

Embracing yourself isn't an easy task. It takes time to realize that you should act how your heart and mind tell you, instead of listening to what other people and society ask of you. Every day seems like a lesson or a new sign to lead me where I should go. I may not know where that is yet, but I know that with passion and empathy I will reach where I belong.

On our way home, Noah and I are silent. His emotions are a mess, but I don't ask. I wait for him to speak. I don't like forcing people to talk. I'd rather wait for them to open up.

"You know I never wanted to work in business," he finally says.

"Oh really? What did you want to do?"

"I'll tell you, but don't laugh."

"Come on, have I ever?"

"A chef," he says, and I am shocked.

"How did you go from being a chef to working in our family business?"

"Well, I am good at what I do. I'm just telling you that I like cooking. It's weird, I know, for a man to like cooking."

"Dude, the best chefs in the world are men. It's only weird in your mind because our fathers will make fun of it."

"Yeah, well, I cook for Sarah."

"Of course you do," I say, raising my eyebrows and winking at him. "Oh, Sarah, I love you so much, I made strawberry cake to eat off each other."

"Shut up," he says and we both laugh.

"I love cooking and food. I think it's a source of happiness. I would love to learn about the science of cooking and maybe open my own restaurant someday."

"You glow when you talk about it. I don't want to sound so cliché, but you do."

"Well, you look radiant when you talk about writing. Do you think we're cowards?"

"I don't know, Noah. We grew up to be what they want. It's frustrating."

"Yeah, I know."

We glow when we talk about something we love – this is something we all know. But how far would we go to capture our dreams? Dreams are real, inside all of us. Some are torn between what they grew up to be and what they want to become. I believe this is just another test. Is it going to be the passion that wins?

Chapter Twenty-Two

Lying here beside him makes me feel like everything is going to be alright. As if the world has never hurt me. As if all dreams can come true. As if I am home. Lying here beside him, smelling his heavenly scent and watching him smile makes my heart flourish. I feel like I am blooming, flower-like. My mind pauses and relaxes. My soul feels so peaceful, even though I know that outside these doors there is a war waiting for me.

I wonder everyday if Adam feels the same way. I know deep down that he must. We are the same human, in different bodies. I love how we merge as one, how connected we feel even when we talk about the most trivial things. This must be what everyone calls an epic love. A love like no other, where two humans connect with their hearts, minds, and souls. Even though I've had a bad experience with every relationship I have ever had—and especially with that boy who took away everything that I am—I have never before felt so healed. It's like my whole past does not exist. The pain I felt has disappeared, and all that is left is its lesson. But I feel no shame.

I lie here with him and feel warm, like coming home. I haven't felt this safe since before my mother left me. I lie here and I feel content and whole, as if I have enough energy and power to conquer the whole world. I don't want to conquer the whole world, though. I just want to conquer him; conquer his love, and everything that he is. I want to be here for every step of the way. I want to see him grow old and frail and grey haired. I want to see him in every detail of every day. For the very first time, I want to share my life with someone; with this beautiful human lying beside me. He is vulnerable only for me. He talks about his deep emotions only to me. He kisses me passionately—only me. He looks at me as if I am a saint (when clearly, I am not). And even though he knows all about my past, he still looks at me as if I am the best, most powerful, and beautiful woman he has ever seen. It scares me. It all scares me so much because I have never experienced a love so profound and true. I know this type of love will endure, but I am constantly scared that I might mess it all up. I don't want him to go. I want him here every second of every day. I am in love with this man so deeply, so passionately. I am devoted.

He looks at me with his beautiful walnut and hazel eyes. "I love you, you know that right?"

He always asks this question as though I might give a different answer each time. But my answer is always, "Yes, I love you too. You know that right?"

We don't have to say it, but we love to say it, as often as we can, every moment when we can. Two empaths deeply in love. What could be more magical, loyal, and true than that?

"Are you going to see your mother?" he asks me.

"Yes, I think so. She texted me yesterday to say that she's coming tomorrow."

"Oh, that's nice. You want me to come with you?"

"No, I think I have to do this alone. I'll make Noah drive me there though."

"Okay, but if you need anything…"

I cut him off and say, "I'll call you. Don't worry, okay?"

"It's hard not to worry, but okay," he smiles.

Most people think love is when a person takes your breath away. But I believe that love is when a person makes you breathe again. Makes you feel reborn. As if the world was suffocating until they came. Adam makes me breathe again, like I wasn't alive before he came. Which is true. I was never alive before him.

"I am so grateful for you."

"Oh, Malikah, I am so grateful for you."

He kisses me, and sleepily lays his head on my chest, wrapping his legs around me as if I am his pillow. Hugging me tightly like a baby boy. It's like he's saying, "All mine; you are my one and only."

I want to be all his, in every way possible.

"How is the book going?" he asks, raising his head from my chest and looking at me. His eyes sparkle and shine like the sun and stars all at once.

"I've just finished the outline—I still have so much to do."

"As long as you're doing it, then take all the time you need. I am so excited to see the book, and so proud of you."

He looks deeply into my eyes as I tell him, "I think I am proud too. I never knew I could take any steps towards actually writing, but here I am."

"My future best-selling author."

"That's ambitious! But, I like the sound of it." I smile, "God, where have you been all my life?"

"Waiting for you to show up."

I kiss him deeply. I inhale his breath and smell his scent. We switch positions and now I am on top of him, kissing him so passionately like it's the end of the world. He kisses me back even more. He moves his hands, stroking my back and pulling me closer to him. I hold his hands and move them lower.

"Malikah, are you sure?" he asks.

"Oh, I have never been more sure of anything in my entire life. Until you." My emotions are overwhelmingly intense and I feel tears in my eyes.

"Oh God, I love you so much."

"I love you more."

I take off my shirt and lean on him as he moves his lips down to my chin, then my neck, kissing and gently biting. I have goosebumps, but I am heating up like I am in an oven.

He raises his arms and I take off his shirt. He is so warm, and so fucking sexy. He looks at me, pausing in the middle of a kiss, and he smiles.

He buries his head in my neck, breathing in deeply. "I love the way you smell. You are like a drug."

I giggle and kiss him as he quickly, expertly releases my bra.

"Oh, that was impressive," I say, smiling.

"Oh, you haven't seen the best part yet."

He brings me even closer until our skins touch. My chest is on his chest. I can feel the warmth of his skin. I can feel a profound, ineffable connection.

We switch positions again and now I am under him. He looks at me as if I am a painting by Leonardo da Vinci or Gustav Klimt or a sculpture by Michelangelo. Without breaking eye contact, he gently pulls down my jeans, and then moves his head down and tugs at my thong with his teeth.

"You are so beautiful, you have no idea."

I am lying on his bed, completely naked. I feel his eyes analyzing every inch of my body as I analyze every inch of his. I sit up and undo his jeans and he takes them off. He kisses every part of me. Forehead, nose, cheeks, lips, then down to my chin, neck, and collar bones. He holds my breasts with both his hands, smelling me all the way down, kissing and licking. Gradually moving down to my belly and then my pubic hair. And then down again, to the softest part of me. He opens my legs and I spread them wide. With his head between my legs, he starts with a simple kiss, and then he licks. I moan deeply. He licks me again, moving his tongue in a way that deserves an Oscar. I can't keep still; I move along with him. I watch him devouring me like a piece of chocolate cake. He puts one hand on my breast. The other holds my legs open. I am wet. I moan more and more with every movement of his tongue. Eating me up and holding me down.

He looks up, still eating me, and his eyes shine. His eyes speak to me. Without speaking a word, his eyes tell me, "You are mine."

He stands up and removes his boxers. Now he is completely naked, I can admire every part of his body. He sits on his knees and I copy him. I kiss him all the way down, just like he kissed me, mapping my way with kisses and simple licks. I put him in my mouth to taste him. He tastes so good; I could do this all day. He puts his hands in my hair and I hear him moan. It's the best sound I have heard in my entire life. He pulls me up back to him.

"I love you. I want you all, all of you, Malikah," he says, breathing heavily.

"I love you," I reply, my breath matching his.

I lie down for him and spread my legs. He leans over me until we are skin to skin. Every part of our bodies is touching. He whispers in my ear, "I want to be inside you so much."

"I want you inside me so much," I whisper back.

I hold him round his waist and pull him hard against me. Then slowly, he invades my insides and we moan. He moves slowly inside of me, gently in and out, scared that I might be hurting. But I am not. He pauses, with all of him inside me, and we sink into this moment. Now we are connected, mentally, emotionally, and physically.

"Oh, can this be my new home? I want to live here," he says, smiling.

"Welcome home then," I say.

I wrap my legs around him and feel him move inside me.

"I want to be on top," I say.

"Control freak mood is on, is it?"

I smile and he lifts me up, but instead of twisting so that I am on top, he pushes me to the wall.

"I am a control freak too sometimes, you know." He smirks and I know he has his lusty Adam mode on.

Still inside me, he moves me up and down. I wrap my arms and legs around him, my back against the wall. It's like a symphony that only we can play. He buries his face in my hair, breathing me in.

He pulls me now, away from the wall, and twists so I am on top, where I want to be. I feel him deep inside, touching all my edges. He moves along with me. "I feel your edges, your pulses, and your cum all over me," he says.

I moan, moving from side to side, and up and down making him touch every side of me. He squeezes my ass and my moaning gets louder—I never knew I could be that loud. But I cannot help it.

Now he moves faster and faster, in and out, up and down. I scream and moan. I cum all over him, soaking his pelvis with my cum and breathing heavily. My whole body is shaking, overwhelmed by the sensation as he cums just a second after me.

I lie there for a while, on top of him. We're both breathing heavily, trying to let intense sensations and emotions sink in. Now I am all his and he is all mine.

"I think I can die peaceful now," he says and I laugh at his expression. "That was just out of this world. What are you?" he asks.

"Your fellow super-empath human," I smile.

"You are so beautiful. I can't believe it."

"Well, you are so beautiful too," I reply.

We share a soft kiss, this time calm with exhaustion. I love him so much.

We lie on the bed naked, cuddling. And then it hits me. I have been ignoring a niggling fear, but I can't ignore it any longer.

All I can think about is how he doesn't live here. He has school back at his home and so many duties. *Don't freak out, Malikah, please. You just had the best sex of your life. Just ask him.*

"When are you going back to London?" I ask, terrified of the answer.

"In few weeks. Maybe, a month," he says. "But I'll be back."

"When?"

"I might spend less time there, since you are here. I'll try to stay there for two or three weeks maximum and then come back here, to you."

"Am I messing up your schedule? What about school?" I ask.

"Honey, I'll rebuild and change my whole schedule for you. You don't have to worry about anything, okay? I am here."

"Okay."

He hugs me tightly and I can smell his heavenly scent. I don't want him to leave. Now I am more attached than ever. I hate when I get too attached, but I love him too much to be away from him for too long. I suddenly panic as I realize just how attached I already am, and that this attachment can only grow more intense. Now he is going to have power over me and I won't be able to control it.

Adam is not the type of person who manipulates but I'm slowly starting to freak out.

"What's wrong?" he asks. He can tell something's up.

"Nothing. I just think I have to go."

"Oh, come on already."

"Yes, I am sorry, love, curfew." I break a smile.

"There is something wrong—I can I feel it."

"I just need a moment to calm down. I think I am too attached to you now and it scares me."

"Malikah, come on," he stands up and hugs me. "I am as much attached as you are. Just breathe."

I try to calm myself down as he hugs me. I put my head on his chest and I breathe. But I know my mind, my fucked-up thoughts and insecurities from the past won't stay quiet for long.

Chapter Twenty-Three

It's 07:00 and someone has turned on the lights in my room. I can't open my eyes, but I know who it is. I hear his angry thoughts.

"Wake up, we have a meeting," he says. He is in complete denial—he refuses to accept that I will not work with him again. In complete denial of the fact that he slapped me twice and never apologized. In complete denial of everything that I am, because for him I am nothing but a submissive child, waiting to be controlled.

"I am not going," I tell him, covering my face with my silk sheets.

"It's not a choice anymore," he replies, pulling off my covers. "I have been so patient with you. I have been so calm so for so long. And don't you tell me that my slapping you hurt, because you deserved so much more for disrespecting me. Now wake up and do your duty." My father looks down at me and his face is red. Someone must have angered him already this morning.

"Did your wife leave you or something, you seem too angry," I ask, but he smiles and me.

"Well, no. But if she did, it would be her loss."

Sure, it will, I say to myself.

"I am not going anywhere with you."

I stand up to face him. I don't want him to think that I am weak or scared. I don't want him to think he has any control over me.

"I have got work to do," I tell him.

"Yeah, like what? Writing a best-selling novel?" he laughs. He is laughing at my hard work and my dream. My passion.

"Oh, it's good to hear that you know your daughter wants to be a writer."

"It's never going to happen. While you are working this out, you need to get dressed."

"No."

"This is an order."

"Well, too bad, because I am not your slave or your puppet. You cannot just move me around how you want."

"Malikah, you don't want to make me cross."

"Father, you don't want to make ME cross. Plus, I am probably going to see Mother today. I'm just waiting for her to text me."

"Are you challenging me?" he glares at me. "You can't see your mother. I forbid you years ago."

"Well, too bad. You have no control over me now."

Noah enters the room. Hearing my father's anger, he stands between us. He holds my father back.

Father suddenly shouts, "If you live under my roof, you abide by my rules."

"Well, then I think I won't live under your roof anymore, dear Father. Leave him, Noah. Maybe he wants to hit me some more. Come on, dear Father, show me what you've got."

He stares at me. His eyes are wide open and stunned. There is silence for a while. After a long pause, he finally tells me to get out of his house.

"Uncle Zayne, just calm down," Noah begs.

"Get out of my house NOW," my father shouts. "Go see your ugly bitch of a mother. You two belong together. You were not meant to be born into the Al-Hadidi family. You were born to be a stubborn young girl. Go be a fucking writer. Show me how you'll do it. I bet you can't do shit without me. I am your salvation and your networks. I was the only one who was there for you. Get out of my fucking house."

I pick up a backpack and pack some random clothes. Noah is still holding my father back.

"Let me go," Father instructs. But instead, Noah walks him through to the living room, leaving me time to pack.

I get dressed as quickly as possible.

"Where the fuck do you think you are going?" Father yells.

"You told me to leave the house."

"Oh, you are not going anywhere."

"I hate you," I tell him calmly. I look him in the eye and I slam the door in his face.

For a moment I've got no idea where to go, but then I remember Bilal who lives downstairs from us.

I knock on his apartment door, two floors down.

"Hey, my dear, what are you doing here? I was just heading off to work."

"Well, my father kind of threw me out the house. Can I stay with you?"

"Threw you out?" Bilal is shocked. "Come in, of course. What happened?" he asks, and I can hear all the affection and care inside of him. He listens carefully as I tell him the whole story.

"God, mentioning your mother must have made him even more mad."

"I don't understand that," I sigh. "I mean, he cheated on her a lot, I know."

Bilal takes a step backwards, surprised. I can hear his shock and confusion. I can tell that there is more to this story.

"Look dear, we don't choose our parents. But we do have to deal with them, because that's just the way it is. Your father thinks he is doing the right thing for you. Nothing will change that. What you have to do is prove him wrong. Pursue your dream, until he realizes that you are perfectly capable of choosing your way."

Bilal is right but it's not that easy. Sometimes I am not even sure if I can achieve my dream. Sometimes when I write, for a moment I feel so happy, and that my hard work will pay off. But other times, I want to smash the whole laptop because I feel like I write so bad and I think maybe I should just stick to the family business.

"You will always doubt yourself, but it's okay as long you keep going," Bilal says, as if he can read my mind. He hugs me and it feels weird, because we have never hugged before.

"You are brave," he tells me. But I start to cry. I am not brave, I am not anything. I am just trying to find my way, I know that.

"Make yourself at home," he says as he lets go of me. As he walks towards the door, he asks, "When did you say your mother is coming?"

"She said she'll text me when she lands. I think it's today."

His emotions turn into missing and love. He suddenly feels this nostalgia and I can see that he's gone into a world of his own.

"Uncle Bilal," I call. "Are you okay?"

"What?" he coughs. "Yes, sure. Why wouldn't I be? Stay safe, kiddo."

He closes the door behind him, but his emotions are still too loud, and I can hear them from outside. There is something weird about this. Something that I don't understand. My phone rings and it's Noah.

"Are you okay?" he asks me, breathing fast as if he's been running.

"Yes! I'm at Uncle Bilal's house."

"Really? I have never been there."

"Yes, me too. It's weird since he is only two floors down. Come and find me?"

Bilal's house is cozy, homey, and very comfortable. It has this contemporary theme with a bit of modern. He has paintings all over the house. It's not as fancy as Father's penthouse, but it has more soul. Bilal's house feels so lonely, though, and I suddenly wonder why he has never married. I walk around his home. It's not a penthouse like Father's or Uncle Jabril's, but it's a huge apartment with so much color.

I could actually stay here and never go back upstairs. I wonder again why someone so handsome, successful, passionate, and kind could be so lonely. Maybe it's because of the girl who broke his heart and left him, or maybe he just likes being alone. Whatever it is, I am glad he is here to take me in and understand me when no one else does.

I hear knocking on the door and I open up.

Noah hugs me. "It's okay. Are you okay?" he asks, worried. He looks like he's almost crying.

"I was coming to you to tell you that Sarah's mother is out of hospital, and feels much better. But then I walked into the middle of your fight."

"Well, I am glad you came before he actually killed me this time," I smile.

"That's not funny. Do you think he'll come for you?"

"Yes, he will for sure. But I won't give in to him. I'm sorry, I'm still trying to process what just happened."

"So, what now?" he asks.

"Now, I write."

Chapter Twenty-Four

I think about all the ways in which I could greet my mother—after all, I haven't seen her for nine years. Will I shake her hand because she is a stranger, or will I throw myself at her and hug her? Will I let out the real, emotional, vulnerable, forgiving Malikah, or will I resent her, be rude to her and make her cry? I have so many personalities, it's hard to choose one. I think we all have different personalities inside us—one for each situation. However, I have never before been so disturbed and worried about something that is only few hours away. Inside me, I want to rip her heart out and soak her with all the anger and agony she built inside me when she left and didn't look back.

But there is a part of me that still remember her vanilla scent and her tangled, curly blonde hair. I still remember the breakfasts she made me every morning; scrambled eggs and hotdogs. Sometimes, she forced me to eat oats, hoping I'd grow up healthy and strong. But when I refused, she'd make me oat cakes with chocolate or peanut butter. I still remember how she would shower me with kisses every night as I went to sleep. I still remember how mad she would get when I was studying math—because neither of us was very good with numbers. She'd say, *Well, you are definitely not going to be a mathematician, are you*? And we'd laugh. I remember my first piano lesson, and how she surprised me by buying me an actual piano. She would sit with her tea and listen to me play something very basic and silly, like "Twinkle Twinkle," but she'd make me feel like I was playing a Beethoven sonata. I stopped playing the piano when she went away. It wasn't something I wanted to do anymore; it reminded me of her.

I still remember how she would burn herself cooking and I'd scream at her as if she was the child and I was the mother. I'd put cream on her burns, and she would say, *You'll make a great mother one day*. I don't want to be a mother anymore. Not since the day she left me. I don't care when someone burns themselves while cooking. Especially me. I remember when she would sing me a song from the '60s or the '50s, or even older, and how I would sing along with her every word. Because, even at the age of seven I would listen to Sabah and Om Kalthom just because Mom loved them.

Now, I don't listen to any of the music she liked, because then I would have to remember all of this. I would have to remember how many times I waited at the door for her, hoping she would come back. I would have to remember how I cried myself to sleep every night as I listened to dear Father fucking other women. I would have to remember every bit I loved and missed about her, and I don't want that. I don't want to remember her or to see her.

In my heart, I hold a grudge against her. She is one of the major reasons that I grew up to be so insecure, so lonely, so messed up. As a child, I thought she left because she hated me. Even when Father told me that she left because of him, I couldn't work out why – why would she leave the whole fucking country? She had me, was I not enough? I am so scared of seeing her, because seeing her will bring back all those insecurities and sad emotions. I hate my mother just as much as I hate my father. I could greet her in a million different ways. But none of them will ever mirror the pain my parents' actions have caused.

It has been six weeks since she text me to say she would be visiting. She is such a coward. She doesn't do confrontation and she never calls me to speak her truth. Instead, she writes it in a text. But then it strikes me that I hate confrontations too. I'd rather write my emotions than say them out loud. But we haven't seen each other in years—surely she could just tell me she loves me, instead of writing it down in a text message? I believe my mother is scared of how I would react. But what I do not get is why the hell did she suddenly decide to see me? Is she wanting to get closer to me? How does her mind even work? I am curious to hear her emotions—her real messed up emotions—because my powers are more powerful now than they have ever been. Once I listened to them, and recognized their value and their worth, my powers fully emerged in all their strength.

I feel my anger washing me from top to toe, fighting with my affection and my compassion. I feel how much I miss having a mother. And in contradiction, I feel how much I hate how this all affects me. I feel my panic rising, but I try to calm myself down; this is no time for panic. I have to be strong, but also empathetic. I just have to be me.

"Okay, we're here," Noah says, parking the car in front of the old house in Garden City—the one that me, Mom, and Dad use to live in when we were a family. I take a deep breath and glance at the house, then look back at Noah.

"Thank you for driving me."

Noah pouts and I know I don't have to thank him. This is one of the most terrifying moments of my life, and he is there.

"You know you don't have to thank me. You are welcome. Now hurry up—go and get to know her."

"Are you going to leave me here?" I ask in panic, trying to keep myself stable.

"I have a date with Sarah. I thought I'd come back for you afterwards."

"No, no. Please don't leave. Can't you wait for me?" I ask. "Look, there is a restaurant just around the corner—you could ask Sarah to come there? And then you guys could wait for me? Please Noah?"

"Of course, of course—just calm down. It's going to be alright, Malikah. It's okay, I am here." Noah hugs me tight and I try to breathe slowly. I need to get this over with.

"Okay," I whisper. "Wish me luck, I guess."

"Good luck, Malikah," he calls after me, and gives me a thumbs up as I get out of the car. I stand in front of my old home for a moment. I inhale the December breeze. I love winter. It's a lovely day. I shouldn't be this scared. She is my mother—why am I so worried?

It's okay, I tell myself.

I am wearing one of my favorite outfits—a short black velvet dress and long lace socks with knee-high boots. My hair is down and I've put some blusher on. I want her to see me as the woman that I am. I've brought my dark burgundy coat with me. It's my favorite, even though Dad bought it. But that doesn't matter right now.

As I enter the building, I notice how old it is. But I still love its old architecture with its high ceilings and wooden floors. Elevators make me claustrophobic, so I take the stairs. I don't need to add to my anxiety right now. We used to live on the fourth floor, so it shouldn't be tiring to climb the stairs. I take a deep breath with every step. Every step that takes me closer to the fourth floor. I pause as I look at the door—the door to my old home. I used to love this house, this building, because it was my home. But now it feels so sad coming here. Father wrote this house over to my Mom when they got divorced. She didn't sell it, but I don't think she ever used it. Being here is making me feel sick.

I approach the apartment door and I find that it is already open and I can see that all the lights are on. Is she really that careless? Who leaves the door open like this? I slowly push the door open. All of our old furniture is covered. The place is not clean and I can see dust everywhere. I cough.

"Mom?" I call out for her. "Are you here?" But there is no answer.

I go to the kitchen, and find that all the appliances have been turned off. There is a cold cup of tea on the table.

"Where the hell did she go?" I whisper. I go to my old room. All my old toys are still there. I see the mermaid sheets on my little bed and the Disney posters on the walls and, despite myself, I smile. There is a picture of me and Mom when I was just a few days old. I take it out of its frame and put it in my pocket. I take another photo too—this one of me, Mom, and Dad.

Remembering my childhood is painful, but this room brings back just a few very good memories, and I try to hold on to them.

I call out for her again, "Mom, are you here?" I take my phone out of my pocket and call her number. I can hear her mobile phone ringing. It's coming from my parents' old room. I approach slowly. I open the door. Oh God. What I see makes me drop to the ground.

"Mom?" I whisper.

I can't breathe, I can't breathe, I can't breathe.

"Mom," I scream, over and over and over again but it doesn't change what I've found. My mother is hanging from the ceiling, a rope wrapped tightly around her neck.

My mother is dead.

She has killed herself on the very day we were due to be reunited. Suddenly I don't care how I would greet her; how I would treat her. Suddenly all the memories seem so far away, all my pain and anger has disappeared. My heart is in flames, and my eyes can't believe what they are seeing.

I'm still screaming, still calling her name.

"Mom!" I scream again. "No. Why? Why Mom, why?" I scream until I can't breathe. I can't move, paralyzed as though I've suddenly forgotten how to function. My whole body is shaking. I feel my phone vibrating and I try to see who is calling. It's Noah.

"Malikah, are you okay? I heard screaming?"

"Noah," I scream. "She is dead, Noah!"

As I drop the phone, I hear him say, "Wait right there, I am coming up."

I try to stand up, but I feel so heavy. "It's okay, I will save you," I tell my mom.

I climb on a chair and try to take off the rope, but it's so tight that it hurts my hand.

"Wait, I will help you. Just wait. No, wait," I talk to myself.

I hear Noah's footsteps. He is running.

"Malikah?" He looks at my mother, then back at me.

"I want to help her. Help me to help her, Noah. Please?" My voice sounds calm, but I am not.

"Oh, Malikah, honey."

"I said, help me, Noah!" I shout at him.

He comes towards me and holds me tightly. Still standing on the chair, I start to kick him.

"Let me go. I am telling you, if you can't help me then please leave." But he just hugs me tighter.

"Breathe, Malikah."

"Don't you fucking tell me to breathe! Can't you see, she needs our help! She must be stuck!" I shout, trying again to remove the rope. I see Noah dialing the emergency number.

"Hello? There has been a suicide," he says.

"What the fuck, Noah? No one has committed suicide here. Fuck you."

"Yes, please come quickly." He hangs up and looks at me. "Malikah."

"What?" I answer, still trying to free my mother.

"Come here, darling. Let me just talk to you," he says, calmly.

"Will you help me after that?" I ask, with tears in my eyes.

"Yes, I will do whatever you want afterwards."

I come down from the chair and he leads me from the room. My body is still shaking, and I have lost the ability to blink. I can't stand on my feet. I feel my legs are getting weak. Noah holds me up; stops me from dropping to the ground. He hugs me tight and I cry my heart out. "It's okay. Let it all out. I am here." Noah strokes my hair.

"She needs help, Noah," I scream as I cry. I cry and I cry, until the police and the ambulance come. Sarah arrives at the same time. I am paralyzed. I cannot talk. I cannot move. I watch them take my mother and cover her body in a black bag.

"That's my mother for god's sake! I want to see her," I yell at the nurses as I rip open the black bag.

I lean in and hug her. I can't smell her vanilla scent. Her curly hair is now so short. Her fair skin is blue and her eyes are so scary, staring dead at me. I close her eyes and look at her face.

"Why, Mom?" I am asking myself, and I'm also asking her. Why did she do it? Why now? Why today? I am desperate for an answer that I know I will never get.

"Are you Malikah?" a police officer asks me.

"Yes, she is," Sarah answers. She is holding one of my hands. Noah is holding the other.

"We found this in your mother's pocket. It has your name on it." He holds out a flash drive. I look at it impassively. Eventually, Sarah takes it and puts it into my purse.

"I am here," she keeps telling me, but I can't respond.

"I called Adam. He should be here soon," Noah says.

But still I can't react.

"Hello, are you a relative of the victim?"

Victim? Did he just call my mother a victim?

"Yes, sir, she is," Noah answers.

"I am Detective Hisham. I am so sorry for your loss. I just have one concern—we better keep this incident quiet. Suicide is taboo; it's a sin. Reporters from everywhere are going to follow this case and build rumors. We don't want that."

"What are you suggesting?"

"Don't tell people it was suicide. We will cover all the tracks. We will pretend it was just a normal death," Detective Hisham says.

"Cover all the tracks? A victim? Taboo and sinful act? Hmm, Detective Hisham, didn't anyone in your fucking family teach you anything about empathy and compassion?" I yell at him.

"Excuse me but that is disrespectful!"

"Disrespectful?" I laugh. "I will tell you what is disrespectful. Disrespectful is people like you coming to people like me in the middle of a horrifying, terrible, miserable incident. An incident that is going to stay with me all my life. This scene is going to be stuck deep in my fucking mind. I won't be able to sleep. I haven't seen my mother for ten years. I was going to see her today. And where is she? Oh yes," I laugh. "She committed the fucking sinful act of suicide. Do you really think she was mentally stable? No one does this when they are in their right mind. Do you have any idea how I feel? Huh? No, you don't! So shut your mouth, if you don't mind, and leave us alone. Let me grieve my mother. The mother I never knew."

My words shock him, scare him even. He leaves without saying a word.

"Malikah?" I hear Adam calling from behind me. I look at him and I'm crying again. He holds me tight against him as I collapse into his arms. I drop and everything fades to black.

Chapter Twenty-Five

Here she is, sleeping peacefully as women gently wash her body so we can bury her in the ground, forever. She has left me again, this time for good. She has left me with the memory of her blue face and her hanging body. I watch them wash her body from a distance, I don't want to join in. I feel like I will get sick if I do. I haven't stopped crying yet. I could fill an ocean with the tears I've cried. My mother has left me again, this time for good. Yesterday, when I got home, I couldn't talk or even breathe. Adam, Noah, and Sarah laid me down on my bed. Father came to see me. He wasn't overly upset. His emotions were relieved. I know he thinks that he was right when he forbid me from seeing her, but what if she did this *because* he forbid me from seeing her for all these years. But then again, I think to myself, she knew I was coming. What the hell happened? This whole thing is a mystery to me. I don't know her. I think I never did.

I approach her body just before they finish washing it. I look at her, she looks like an angel. Her skin is so white, and her hair looks so beautiful now. *Oh Mother, I wish I knew you.*

"I want to go outside," I say.

"Okay dear, let's go," Sarah replies with all her empathy. She has been holding my hand since yesterday, not letting me go. And among this misery, I am feeling grateful for her.

We get into Noah's car and start driving to the cemetery. I fall asleep, my head resting on Sarah's shoulder, I haven't slept since yesterday. We reach the cemetery in what it seems like two minutes, but it actually took us two hours. We all stand as they take out my mother's body, to put her in the ground. Then it all hit me. I am never, ever going to see her again.

"Mom," I scream, trying to run towards the hole they have dug for her. But Noah holds me. "Leave me!" I scream in his face, stamping on his feet with as much power as I can, so I can hurt him. He groans and lets me go. I jump into the hole, with her body.

"Please no, don't leave me. No. Not again," I cry. "What did I ever do? Why did I deserve this? Didn't you love me at all?" I scream, "Mom."

Adam leans down from above me and holds out his hand. "Malikah, it is alright. Come on, hold my hand. I am here."

"No, leave me here. I want to stay with her," I cry.

"I'm afraid that isn't possible, my love. She needs her peace. Can you give her that?"

I look at him and nod.

"Alright then, to give her peace, she must be buried. You can pray for her as much as you like. This will give her peace. Would you like that?"

"Yes," I whisper. "But I don't want to leave her!" I cry.

"I know, my love, but this is just the way it goes. Come up here and we'll talk about it. I am here. You know I am here."

"Yes, alright. Can I just hug her?" I ask.

"Of course, I'll wait."

The hole is full of insects and I can see a couple of rats, but I don't care. She is covered with a white sheet, but I don't care. The hole smells like dead humans, but I don't care. I sit on the ground and lean in to hug her.

"I love you even though you left me; even though I don't know you," I whisper. I start to cough. "I don't know why you did this, but I forgive you for leaving me again. Even though, in my mind, I never thought I could."

"Come on, Malikah. Come here now, my love," I hear Adam calling me.

I let go of Mom, and take Adam's hand. He pulls me up from the hole and holds me close.

"Did Father come?" I ask.

"No, I'm afraid he did not," Adam tells me. "But we're all here." He breaks into a smile. He knows I am disappointed. I mean, even though Mom and Dad weren't good together, it makes me so angry he hasn't bothered to come, not even for me.

"Come on, let's get home," Sarah says, taking my hand. "I'll help you take a shower, okay?"

I nod, I can't speak now. I have lost the ability to express myself. I feel like my mind has been glitching, and my tongue is as heavy as steel. I feel my heart breaking into million pieces and my mind is about to explode. I feel like I want to sleep so bad, but I don't know if I will ever get a good night's sleep again. The four of us get back into Noah's car again and drive to the penthouse.

"I can't see," I tell them. "I can't see!" I scream.

"Noah? Sarah? Adam? Are you there?"

Sarah holds my hand and strokes my hair. "Breathe, it's just from the panic and the pressure. You *can* see."

"No, I can't!" I shout. Sarah is so calm, trying to deal with my psychological breakdown. I feel her worry, but she is also confident that she can help me. After all, she is a psychologist.

"I'll tell you what, why don't you lie your head on my lap and close your eyes for a while? It has been a hard day. Can you do that?" she asks me politely.

"Don't you fucking treat me like a patient! I am telling you, I have lost my sight!"

I am shaking, and my head is spinning. I feel unstable—like I am on a roller coaster. I can't breathe and I feel paralyzed. Sarah holds my shaking body. "It's going to be alright," she says.

"How the fuck do you know? You don't have a clue what I feel!" I scream. "I can't breathe. I need air, please. Open the windows."

I have lost my sight, I can't see anything, I am having a panic attack for the third time in two days.

I hear Adam ask Noah to stop the car. "What?" Noah answers.

"Stop the car here. I need to get her out, trust me," Adam replies.

Noah parks the car at the side of the high road. I hear Adam get out of his passenger seat and open my door.

"Come on, I will hold you now, okay?"

I nod. He takes my hands and holds me up so I can walk.

"We are on a high road, in the middle of nowhere. You feel like you lost your sight, you are having a panic attack. Is that correct?"

I nod and try to breathe.

"I haven't told you this before, but you know why I never talk about my past or my family?"

"No," I whisper. "What does that have to do with anything? Are you crazy?"

He holds my head. He is tall, and I only come up to his shoulder.

"My mother, she overdosed on pills. She did it because she wanted to die. She committed suicide. I was twelve years old. I know how you feel, Malikah," he whispers in my ear.

I open my eyes and I finally can see. I look at him. "What?"

"Let's go home. I will tell you all about it, and you can tell me all about what happened to you too." Adam sighs, then says, "I told you, I am here for you, okay?"

"Okay," I whisper.

He kisses my forehead and opens the car door for me. We get in the car and I lie back on Sarah's lap. I try to sleep again, but I can't. Now all I can think about is how little twelve-year-old Adam lived through this painful experience. I am twenty-one years old and already I'm out of my fucking mind. I took out my hip flask, which is filled with Whisky, and take two sips. It burns me as I haven't eaten for two days. No one comments, because they know I'll drink it anyway. What if all of this is just a sign that I am doing everything wrong? What if this is the sign that is sending me back to my father, before I lose him too? What if this whole thing is nothing but proof that I should just stick to what I should have grown up to be? My mind drifts away in thoughts, until I can no longer hold my head up, and I drop into Sarah's lap once more.

Chapter Twenty-Six

Today, the funeral went just like any funeral would. People I don't know passing by me, shaking my hand and giving me their condolences. No one knows she committed suicide. So whenever anyone asks what happened I just start to cry automatically. My father told me no one should know, just like the police officers did. He said it would shed too much light on our family and start too many rumors.

I didn't argue. I don't have the energy anymore. I look at the ground, and try to get through this funeral without breaking down. My thoughts are still paralyzed. Everything inside my mind is glitching—like a computer error or a child's toy with almost dead batteries. I just stand there, like a statue shaking hands, saying thank you. I didn't know all these people knew my mother. But then again, it turns out that I don't know anything about her. Everyone tells me how great she was, how much she helped people, how much love she had to give.

They all say, "We don't know what happened or when she moved to London, she just disappeared." And they look at me as if I know the reason, as if I know why she disappeared. Well, I don't know, so all I say is "thank you," to pass each moment as politely, and as calmly, as possible. I have only slept for two hours since it happened, and my body is exhausted. No one from my family came, except for Noah.

"Miss Malikah, did you listen to what I said?" Mr. Tommy asked.

"What? No, I'm sorry," I apologize.

Tommy sighs, "Look, Miss Malikah, I know you are going through a terribly hard time but I came all the way from London to give you what your mother has left for you. It has been a hard week, I understand. But please listen to what I have to say. It's your mother's will."

"Sure, I am so sorry. Continue please."

"Okay, so your mother's house in London will certainly pass to you. She had no sisters or other living family members. There is just you." Tommy looks at the papers and passes them to me for my signature. "These are her keys, and here is the address of her apartment in London. If you don't want anything to do with the apartment, since you live here, I can help you communicate with some real estate agents to help you sell it."

"Sure, I will think about it. But I think I'll keep it for now."

"Very well, then we shall continue. According to your mother's will, she left you an unopened letter. She told me that if anything happened to her, you should receive this letter when you reach twenty-one years of age. Of course, she altered the letter few times, but this is the final copy."

He hands me a letter.

"Did you read it?" I ask.

"No, I'm afraid that wouldn't have been appropriate—she said it should be read only by you. There is another thing; a flash drive. But I can't seem to find the original one."

"Yes, the police officer found it in her pocket," I remember.

"Oh, okay she must have taken it with her. Well, anyway, I said I would make a copy of it just in case, and here it is."

"Thank you."

Tommy's emotions are empathetic toward me, he must know that it has been years since I've seen Mom. Inside, he feels sorry and apologetic, but he is trying to maintain a professional image. I already like him. He seems nice.

"Well, if you have any trouble with any of the papers, let me know. And if you are planning to change your mind about the apartment, just get in touch. This is my card." He hands me his card and says, "My condolences to you, Miss Malikah, may your mother rest in peace. She was a lovely woman. So, kind and understanding." He is smiling.

"Well, thank you, Tommy. I wouldn't know about that. I didn't have the chance to know her." I try to break into a smile, but I know I have made him sad. It must be hard to deal with people in situations like this.

Tommy and I shake hands, and I escort him to the door just as Bilal shows up. He looks awful, his eyes and his face are red, like he has been crying.

"Are you okay?" he asks me. "Can you tell me what happened?"

There is so much urgency in his voice.

"I need to calm down please, it has been a tough week," I say, motioning for him to come in.

"It's okay, you don't have to talk then. Let's just hang out." I feel his voice tremble. He feels like he wants to cry.

"Are you always this emotional? Why do you feel like crying?"

"What? No, I am just so worried about you," he says, but this is only partly true. There is more. He feels like his heart has been broken. Like he has lost his soul.

"I am sorry, but I need to sit alone for a while. I already sent Noah, Sarah, and Adam away. They will come back later. Maybe you can do the same?"

I don't want to hear another person's emotions today.

"Oh, okay then. I'll see you later."

I can feel his disappointment and his sadness, but I let him go. I have had enough, and I can't tolerate anyone at all right now.

I don't have the ability or the strength to open either Mom's letter or the flash drive. I just want to lie back for now and sleep until Friday's dinner has been and gone. But sadly I am forced to attend.

At the table, everyone is eating and having conversations. I look at my food, trying to eat anything at all.

"So, Malikah, when are you coming back to work?" Father asks.

I take a deep breath. "My mother just died! Where is your compassion?"

"Yes, dear, I am sorry—but you never knew her anyway?" he looks at me, smiling.

"Is this your idea of calming me down?" My voice is starting to rise.

"Sorry, calm down! Sorry, okay. Just eat. Whenever you're good, we'll talk." He is scared that I may explode at any moment.

"What did the lawyer say then?" Father asks.

I sigh and tell him about the letter and the flash drive and her house in London.

My father almost chokes, and he suddenly feels worried. "Hmm. And did you open any of these things?"

"No, not yet."

Karma smiles and says, "Oh be careful, Uncle Zayne—she must have her mother's crazy gene."

The whole room falls silent. Sarah and Noah look at each other in shock. Father almost chokes again. Jabril coughs and stares at his daughter, but I feel him laughing inside.

"What? I am kidding! It's a joke!"

I stand up and pour a glass of icy cold water into a large cup. I walk around the table until I'm standing next to Karma. And then slowly, deliberately, I pour the whole cup over her head. She screams. No one moves and no one tries to stop me.

"My mother's crazy gene? You spoilt little bitch. I hope you fucking die."

Karma's fear rises. I have never before taken any actions toward her. I usually just let her talk and make fun all she wants, but this time I am not letting anyone do shit.

"And you." I look at Father. "Don't you dare talk to me about work. I hate your job, I hate this house. I hate this life and I hate you," I scream in his face. "You forbid me from seeing her, and now look what she did! It's all because of you."

He is stunned and shocked, trying to manage his emotions, trying to stop himself from getting angry.

"Well, I didn't realize that I caused her ill mind," he replies.

I laugh. "Ill mind? We are all ill-minded, Dad. We are all mentally ill in one way or another. Being mentally ill doesn't mean you are crazy, it just means that certain types of trauma or incidents affect you in a different, more extreme way. I am ill, you are ill, Karma is definitely fucking ill. We all are. Do you think she is crazy because she committed suicide? No, Dad, the whole world affected her in ways you can't even imagine. That's why people decide to end their lives—not because they are crazy, but simply because they *feel* so very fucking much.

"It's not the right choice, I give you that. But what does this country or even the whole fucking world do to try to fix it, huh? The world just keeps getting worse and worse. I have no words for it. You are a narcissist. Karma is just a fucking egoistic, insecure, self-absorbed bitch. Jabril is a jealous, envious, and secretly evil person. Bilal is the kindest and most emotional man, but he has trust issues and can't talk to anyone. Noah is perfection—possibly too perfect, meaning he sometimes obsesses over things. Sarah, well, she is a psychologist and that makes her hard to analyze, but even she has low self-esteem at times." I pause and look at Father as he sits next to his wife. "And all your fucking wives are whores who are just with you for your money." I laugh. "And me? I am the most fucked up person of all time. I have a superpower that I can't embrace. I am so tired of hearing your fucked-up emotions, I am passive when I shouldn't be and angry all the time. I am depressed, obsessed, and lonely. I am a fucking pleaser and I hate that so much. I am insecure and I don't trust easily. I am mad at this world. And I'm even more mad at myself, because I know I have the powers to change things, but I don't do shit. But you know what? This will change."

I leave the room. I leave them all silent and uncomfortable, breathless and scared, confronting their own truths. I leave them and go to my bedroom, pack the letter, the flash drive, and my laptop. I take off, without telling anyone where I'm going. But I am not coming back until I have had the courage to open the letter and the flash drive. I have a strong feeling that this letter will lead me to myself. I don't know why I feel this—but it's a really strong feeling deep down inside of me. I need to be brave. I need to face my own truth this time.

Chapter Twenty-Seven

When I hug him, I feel safe. It's like everything is going to be alright. When I hug him, I feel like I'm home—a feeling I've been deprived of all my life. I don't believe in happy endings—that's why I freak out every time I feel too much for him. But he is the only person who will understand me. I sit on the couch, holding my bag in my arms like it's a baby that I'm too scared to let go of. Adam has made me hot tea and has given me a blanket. He is trying to calm me down.

"I understand," he repeats, whenever I talk about what I did; what I said. I tell him how bad I feel for hurting others. But it's just not something I can hold in any longer. I can't be sad, passive, depressed Malikah anymore.

"Will you tell me about your mother?" I ask. He sits back down and looks up at the ceiling. I can't listen to his emotions, but I know this must be a terrifyingly hard question to answer.

"It's okay if you don't want to," I say quickly, trying to save the moment. I don't want him to feel sad.

"No, it's fine." He takes a deep breathe before jumping into his ocean of pain, memories, and fear. He talks without looking at me. He just stares at the ceiling. I realize why he doesn't want my eye contact—it's just so emotional for him to talk about this.

"My father was abusive," he tells me. "My mother had no one but her best friend, who soon traveled to London to complete her studies." He keeps going. He remembers everything, every detail of every painful day as if it was yesterday. He was six years old when he first witnessed his father's cruelty towards his mother. He listened to him hit her over and over again. "I was just a little kid, you know? What could I possibly do at the age of six?" His mother didn't want to leave his father, worried that he would take Adam away from her, so instead she waited. She tolerated. She tried her best to give Adam what he needed. "And she was the perfect mother, honestly, but it killed me. I knew exactly what she felt, the voices told me, and it was hard to talk about it because who would believe a six-year-old kid claiming he has superpowers?" he smiles.

"You know, I always say the same thing about myself. Why would someone believe a crazy lady?" I smile back at him.

He looks at me seriously, "You are not crazy, don't say that, please."

He leans his head back once more and continues his story. Years passed and he grew up eventually to stand up to his father. He was twelve years old the first time he ever stood up to him. He was twelve years old when his mother figured out that he had been silently suffering with panic attacks. "Why would I tell her that I feel panic every night? She was suffering enough. You know." He paused. "Well, I remember that day very vividly. I was trying to sleep, because it was a school night, but I couldn't. He hadn't come home yet and I knew that when he came home late like this, he would be in a terrible mood. He came banging on the door—he'd forgotten his keys. My mother opened the door for him, and he started yelling. He was drunk as hell, his face like the devil, full of anger, resentment, and hate. He started breaking glasses and anything else that came to hand. Mother sat on the floor, trying to save herself from the crazy bastard. He forced her to stand up and then he slapped her face so hard that she fell back to the floor. I ran out of my room and shouted, 'Hey, get your hands off her!' I was just a skinny kid but I didn't care. I just wanted him to get his hands off her. Then he came after me. He pinned me down and started hitting me with his belt. I kept telling him that it didn't hurt, making him even angrier. I mean, I'd rather be in pain myself than watch my mother suffer." He stopped and then looked at me. "I pushed him—hitting both his knees as hard as I could until he fell over. My mother took me away that day. We went to her best friend's house—she had the keys.

"Her best friend came home from London the next day, to stay with Mom. A few days later, Mother told me she was going to our house, to bring the rest of our clothes. So that we could leave for good. But she didn't come back. Without telling Mom's friend Lina where I was going, I went all the way back to our house. I thought Lina may try to stop me." I see tears coming from his eyes, pouring down his beautiful face. "I found her on the floor. She had overdosed on antidepressives. No one was home, not even the bastard who calls himself my father. I was the one who found her, and I broke down, right next to her body. I didn't know what to do. A few hours later, Lina found me. Apparently, Mom had planned it all along. I don't know, depression is not easy." He exhales, as if he has been holding his breath all the way through the story. He holds my hand and says," It's painful when you lose someone. And it's even more painful when you lose someone to suicide. I don't know, and I will never know if my mother had planned it all along. But I do know that she suffered with depression all her life. I was her hope, but she gave me to Lina and Lina took care of me like a mother. I am still sad, and I still feel pain whenever I remember. It's always at the back of my head, you know? But that's why I help people with my powers. Depressed people need empathy; they need someone who will listen and be there. Someone who will help them heal. I've helped people my whole life. It makes me feel like I am keeping my mother's legacy alive, if that makes sense? I also love sports for the same reason—it makes me feel alive. Just like writing makes you feel alive too." He breaks into a smile and wipes his tears.

"I love you so much, you know that?" I tell him.

"I love you too, Malikah."

Losing someone is hard enough, but losing someone to a depressing mental illness that leads to suicide is even harder. You feel like you could've been there, and you start questioning whether you weren't there for them, or didn't listen enough. You can't blame yourself for that. I believe just like Adam that empathy can heal all. How can you find empathy in a land where people are so occupied with themselves, and their needs? In a land where people refuse to communicate or try to understand. How can you find empathy in a land where looks and material possessions are more important than the heart and real, intimate communication? This world needs a new perspective, this world needs hope. But before I try to heal anyone or be the hero of this story. I must first heal myself.

Adam goes to wash his face and answer some calls from his aunt. I wish I could meet the woman who raised such a beautiful man. I lie back on the couch and open my bag. I pull out the letter, take a deep breath as I open it, and start to read.

Dear Malikah,

I am sorry things ended this way. You know I have changed this letter more times than I can count. But I think this is the last time I will change anything in it. Right now, my heart is pounding so fast, because it scares me that you are going to read this. But since you are 21 years old now, I think it's time for you to know the truth. You were the miracle I fought for all my life. You gave me hope when I had nothing. You were, and always will be, my one true love. I know you might find this hard to believe, since I left when you were just a little child. But I couldn't stay. When me and your father got married, we were young and deeply in love. That's what I thought at least, until we realized that I am incapable of getting pregnant. It was a depressing shock, leading me to a downfall that I still haven't gotten over. Your father turned out to be a womanizer. Even after years of love, he would go out and sleep with other women. And it was even worse when we realized that we couldn't have babies. I had no one, no family and nothing. I fought the whole world to marry your father, and in return I lost everyone. Even my family who then years later died one by one. You were just a little child then, and you won't remember your grandparents. But you were the reason they got to talk to me again.

One day, exactly a year before you came, me and your father got into a fight and I left the house. I stayed at a hotel for a while, and the only one who was truly there for me was your Uncle Bilal. Me and Bilal fell in love—the most forbidden love of all. We didn't announce it or act on it, but we knew it was there and your father found out. We completely denied it, but he always felt there was something wrong. We remained separated for two months and we were going to get a divorce. Then one day your father came to me and told me that he had got a twenty-two-year-old woman pregnant. He had started to panic, but then suddenly I had this idea. I went to this woman—who in later years became my therapist. I convinced her to give me her child. I told her my story, and I convinced your father that in this way we would be able to revive the love we had and build a real family. The woman was so young. She was pretty self-absorbed and unreliable, and she certainly didn't want a baby. She had her career in London to pursue, and a whole other life. We tried to give her a lot of money, but the day she had you, she refused to take anything and told us that maybe this angel would save our lives. All three of us signed NDAs, and no one outside the circle knew anything. Except for your Uncle Bilal, who I'm sure still holds the secret. I was so happy to finally have a baby daughter of my own. I loved you because I am your mother and that never changed. But you grew up to look exactly like Lina. You were like a copy and with time it got harder and harder. I would wake up every day realizing that no matter what I did, you are not my flesh and blood. But I still loved you, just as you are. Me and Bilal kept communicating like friends. Nothing ever happened between us, but your father found out we were still talking. And from that day he didn't stop abusing me, even though I was truly trying to revive the love we had. Something broke inside both of us. You were gluing the missing pieces back together, but the puzzle broke anyway. Your father wanted me gone, but I couldn't go and leave you. But then you had your first panic attack, and I felt like it was because of me. I thought I had caused it, and that maybe if I wasn't around, you would be more stable. I started getting depressed. When I left, hoping you'd be better without me, I got even more depressed. I ran away when I shouldn't have. I thought I was saving you from a failed relationship. Saving you from my depressed soul. I thought I was saving you from myself. But I think I killed us both in the process. I couldn't tolerate your father's abusive ways, I became self-destructive and when you witnessed your father's abuse, I hated myself even more. Your father loved you, and I loved you. I am sorry my child for my awful ways. I am sorry you were born into this mess. I am sorry I left you, but believe me it was all for you. I fought to bring you into this world. I fought to be your mother, but your father didn't let me and then my depression arrived. One day, you put your little hand against my chest and you healed me for a while. I knew that day that you must have a special gift. I longed for those little hands that must be all grown up now. I longed for your kisses and hugs. I missed your voice and the way you called my name every minute of every day. Your father forced me to leave, and my depression convinced me that it was for the best. I hope it was all for the best. You saved my life more times than I can remember, even when you weren't with me. I have waited until you came of age, before telling you the truth, so that you would be free to choose what you want out of this life. On the flash drive there are some recordings from my therapy sessions, so that you will maybe understand that I am not just another crazy person. Hopefully you can understand that I loved you. Hopefully you will understand that I have spent ten years all alone, without anyone. I hoped that maybe we could be together someday, but then your father forbid you from seeing me. He must have thought that I was crazy, like anyone else would.

If you go to my house in London, you'll find your photos everywhere. To start with, Bilal kept in contact with me every few months to tell me everything about you that he knew. But this contact stopped because it was hard for both of us to be in each other's lives after I left, especially when he realized that my heart only belongs to you. He loved you deeply too, even without you knowing. You saved my life. And you saved your true mother's life, because she has changed from a self-absorbed, selfish person into a giver and a mother. I don't regret fighting to have you, because you were a miracle. I hope you forgive me and understand that I could not control my illness, or your father, or my miserable life. And I could not stop your father forbidding you from seeing me. I am sorry for everything.

I hope you know I love you. I started loving you from when you were just a fetus, growing in another woman's body. You saved me every day, and I am so sorry I left the way I did. Life is hard my child, and without purpose it becomes meaningless.

*The name of your biological mother is **Dr. Lina Morgan**. You will find her home address, number, and her office address on the back of this letter.*

I put down the letter. I feel the world spinning, I need to breathe. I stand up and stumble to the kitchen, taking a water bottle from the refrigerator and drinking it down in one gulp. I lose my balance and fall to the ground. I can't breathe. This is just too much to take in. My whole life is built on a lie. I wasn't supposed to be born in the first place. I am a mistake, and a sin.

Adam runs towards me, shouting, "Malikah? Oh God what's wrong?" He pulls me up and sits me on the couch. I suddenly recognize the name Lina Morgan. Adam said his aunt, or his mother's best friend, is called Lina. I look at him and ask, "What did you say your mother's best friend's name is? The woman who raised you?"

I see him swallow. He has suddenly started to sweat. "Lina Morgan. Why?"

"Did you know?" I ask calmly.

"Know what?"

"Did you fucking know?" I shout.

"Know what?" he repeats.

"That Lina Morgan is my real mother?" I shout.

"Malikah, I can explain."

Oh no. Oh God no. I try to breathe slowly. "You fucking knew all this time and didn't say anything? You are a liar just like all of them. You helped cover up the fact that my whole life is built on a fucking sin, and a lie. That my cheater father just magically had a miracle baby. I trusted you, Adam, I trusted you," I scream and start to cry hysterically, repeating, "I trusted you."

"Malikah, please! Let me explain. I came here to tell you, but then I found out that you are just like me. I got selfish and I wanted to know you. I fell for you, Malikah, and I didn't know how to tell you all of this. And then when your mother died—" He takes a deep breath. "I knew she would leave you something. That she would tell you. I waited so you would know from her, and then maybe you'd understand."

"Understand? Are you out of your mind? I am not going to believe any shit you say." I stand up, pack my laptop, the letter, and the flash drive. "I regret even coming here. For some reason, I thought you would be trustworthy, just because you are an empath."

"I am trustworthy, it's just—" he paused.

"Yes, that's what I thought too. You can't say anything about this, you are a liar. You will lie even more."

"You are no saint either, Malikah. You have got to listen to my side of the story."

"I don't have to listen to any shit coming out of your mouth." I go to the door as he grabs my hand.

"Please just listen to me," he begs.

"No, Adam. No more." I forcefully remove my hand from his, and close the door behind me.

I woke up this morning with a father and a dead mother, believing that my name was Malikah Zayne Al-Hadidi, daughter of Zayne Al-Hadidi and Dahliah Eissa.

Now my whole life is a lie. My mother is not my mother. My true biological mother gave me away, and my father is a narcissistic, self-absorbed liar. My uncle used to love the woman I thought was my mom, the woman I used to miss so much and who has now committed suicide. The only person I have truly loved in my whole miserable life has turned out to be a liar.

Great, Malikah, your whole life is just another lie.

Chapter Twenty-Eight

As I go back to the penthouse, I feel nothing but anger. It soaks me from head to toe. No one is going to stop me now. No one is going to be safe from precious Malikah, because precious Malikah is not going to hide or be so kind anymore. "Fatma, where is Father?"

"On the roof, dear," Fatma says, smiling at me. Poor Fatma has no idea what I am about to do. "Call the fire fighters then, because I am going to burn this whole penthouse down." I smile back at her and leave.

"What?" she asks, but I don't reply.

I go to my room and grab a big pile of branded clothes that my dear father bought for me. I take them up onto the roof and throw them on the floor in front of him.

"What's going on?" Father asks. I throw my mother's letter at his face.

"Read this, dear father, that's what's going on."

I stand and watch him as he reads the letter. His expression changes, and his emotions turn from confidence to terror. He looks up at me and I can see that he has started to sweat. He takes a step towards me, but I quickly stop him.

"Oh no, keep your distance. I am the one who is going to do the talking now."

"Malikah, you were hope for all of us," he says.

"Oh, was I?" I laugh. "Let me tell you about hope, Daddy," I say sarcastically. "Hope is what you took from me when I was just a child and you forbid me from seeing my mother. Hope is what you took away when I finally had the courage to pursue my passion for writing. Hope is what you burned inside of me when I was just a little girl, having to cope with your disgusting ways with women. Hope is something I've never had. I've never felt it, or experienced it. At least, not as purely and honestly as I should." I pause. "Hope is nowhere near you. You take the oxygen out of any room. You take the hope out of any soul. You care only about yourself. I hate my job and I will never, ever be a part of your company. I hate you and I will never believe anything you say ever again. You have never been a true father. I waited for years, but unfortunately you are just the biggest disappointment, not me. You thought you could buy me with your money; buy me with your fancy clothes and fancy dinners. I wanted a father, not a fucking bank account. And, oh God who can forget how you slapped my face because I wasn't your ideal daughter? My whole life is built upon a lie, it's built upon a sin and a mistake you made years ago with a woman who I now know to be my true mother. You fucked up two women's lives. How very noble of you. Quite the perfect man. All hail the patriarchy we live in. You are such an animal." I start to laugh and I can hear his fear and worry rise. "I have spent my whole life wondering who I am, and why my own mother left me. She was sick and you weren't there for her—in fact, you made it even worse. I now know why you are so jealous of Bilal—it's because he gave her the things you couldn't; love, loyalty, and trust. She may be dead; she may have lied, but she was the only one who wanted to keep me alive. As much as I hate being alive now, I am grateful for her efforts to let little miracle baby Malikah live. You are not just the worst father in the whole god damn universe, but you are the worst human I have ever met. You are beyond helping, beyond fixing. Because nothing can fix that ugly heart of yours."

I smile and light a match. "Boom, there goes your money and your love, Father," I say slowly as I throw the match onto the pile of clothes and watch them catch fire. "You have no idea how I feel now. You will never understand, because you are too self-absorbed. But I hope one day you will regret it all and I hope that for once—man, just for once—you will feel and care about someone other than yourself. Until then, you're not going to see me again."

I walk towards the roof door. I can feel Father is starting to panic. The fire alarm starts ringing. "Malikah, wait," he shouts after me.

I look back at him, but he remains silent. "You have nothing to say, and I have somewhere to be."

"I am your father, listen to me."

"Not anymore."

Noah, Bilal, Jabril, and Karma have heard the alarm, and all come rushing up the stairs. I look at them, but I don't react. I walk past them, straight to my room, with Noah following.

"What the hell happened, Malikah?" His voice is loud and worried.

"I can tell you on the way," I say, packing my bag.

"On the way where?" he asks in surprise.

"London. Now, are you going to pack or not?"

He stands in front of me with a huge question mark on his face. But even though he has no idea what's going on, he feels it's better to be with me. He nods and rushes to his penthouse to pack his bag.

"What the hell is this?" Bilal comes into my room, holding my mother's letter. I snatch it away from him.

"This is none of your business."

"Oh, it absolutely *is* my business," he replies. I can hear his anger, and how disturbed he is by the fire, Mom's letter, and her suicide.

"Just leave me alone." I grab my backpack and push him from the room. I feel his disappointment and his pain but well, it's nothing compared to what I am feeling right now. Luckily there is a bank down in the building foyer. I go to the ATM and withdraw equivalent of £30,000 from my father's account. Noah comes down to find me and Sarah is with him.

"Where did you come from?" I ask Sarah.

"Well, I wasn't going to let you go on your own. Plus, I was already half-packed."

"Why were you half-packed?"

"We were going on a day trip tomorrow," Noah replies.

"Oh shit, I've ruined your weekend. I'm sorry."

"Don't say that!" they reply together.

"We're here for you, whatever it is. Okay?" Sarah says.

"What were you doing?" Noah asks.

"Well, dear Noah, I think I just stole my father's money."

I smile and they both frown, not understanding what I mean.

"I will drive. You read this letter."

I give Noah the letter and hop into my car. Noah gets into the passenger seat and Sarah climbs into the back. They read the letter together, word for word. I hear their emotions change from neutral to anger, then shock and then finally sadness.

"Wait, her name is Lina Morgan?" Sarah asks.

"Yes, look here." Noah answers, pointing at the name.

Sarah leans back. "Guys, she is my scholarship doctor. The one who chose me."

We all fall silent. My world just gets darker and darker every time this woman's name comes up.

"What do you know about her?" I ask.

"Oh Malikah, she is such a lovely woman. She does charity work and heals people in need for free. She also has this treatment center for people with depression—she owns it with her son."

"She has a son?" I ask.

"Well, not precisely, she told me he is her best friend's son. But she raised him as her own after her best friend died."

"Did she tell you his name?"

"Yes, it's Adam, I think."

They both realize it at the same time.

"Adam?" Noah says.

Sarah screams. "Your Adam?" she asks.

"Don't call him 'My Adam' anymore."

I can hear their disappointment, pain, and anger. I wanted to go away on my own, but having them with me makes me feel safe. They are the only people I can trust in this whole damn world. We remain silent all the way to the airport. Sarah caresses my shoulders every few minutes. She has no words to say, but this is how she assures me that she is here. Noah on the other hand is completely still. It's like he can't work out how he feels. Luckily, I am an empath and I hear his pain and worry. I hear how much anger he now has toward every member of the family.

Finally he says, "Well, I've got your back."

"I know."

We park the car and run to the airport door. We wait for an hour, trying to buy tickets to London. But there is only one plane leaving soon and it has only one empty seat. The next one isn't for another two hours.

"I can't wait. I have got to go," I tell my friends.

"Can't you just wait? Then we'll all go together," Noah asks.

"I can't keep calm now, after everything I've learned. I'll take this plane. You book onto the next one. I will text you the address for Mom's house. I have to go. I can't sit still anymore."

"I understand, we will be right after you," Noah reassures me.

"Okay. I love you guys." I hug them both and rush to the boarding gate.

I'm too scared, too afraid but nothing can stop me now. I can't sit still or keep calm as long as I feel like there are pieces missing from my life. Pieces that I have no idea about. The only seat left on the plane is in business class. After take-off, I plug the flash drive into my laptop. I'm hoping that this won't set off another massive truth bomb in my head.

On the flash drive there are pictures of me and my mother when I was young. Pictures I can't remember. There is also a picture of my mother and another woman, who I assume must be Lina.

There are only two recordings. I open the first one.

"How do you feel about letting her go?" someone asks.

"An inexplicable pain," my mother replies.

"What would you tell her, if she was here?" the mystery woman asks.

"I would tell her I am sorry for everything. I would want her to meet her real mother. I would want her to know the

truth, and the fact that I fought for her to be born. I am not the bad guy here, Lina," my mother says.

The other voice is Lina's!!!

"Well, you could try writing her a letter?"
"She can't know about this until she is twenty-one. Until then, she can't make her own decisions. You know how middle eastern men are. He would force her to stay. She wouldn't be able to do anything. She basically has no rights at all until she reaches the legal age."
Lina sighs and says, "You are brave to have come here. I still can't believe you chose me to be your therapist."
"Well, I knew you would understand—as you are involved."

Mother goes on and on about how much she misses me, and about what she would do if she had the chance to see me. She talks about Bilal, calling him "the kindest and the truest one in the family." She claims that she never acted on the love they shared, because she knew she wasn't stable and because it felt wrong.

However, my father cheated on her many times, until I came to the world and he tried to become a good father and a good husband. But then later, when he discovered Bilal's feelings toward my mother, he got angry and he never trusted her again.

"He had a point," she says. "But we had a daughter. I wouldn't act on emotions that would lead to the end of our family. Sadly it ended anyway when he started abusing me— even though I never ever gave Bilal hope or even any suggestion that our feelings for each other would ever amount to anything. I told him many times that it was wrong and that we should be just friends, but well Zayne found out anyway and he thought that I cheated and I really, really didn't. After he started abusing me, I thought Malikah's life would be better if I wasn't there. He used to be a great father."

"But you said you hated that she grew up looking like me," Lina says.

"Yes, I did. It made me feel like an outcast. Like I didn't deserve her. Each year that passed, the thought grew in my mind that sometimes I felt like I was just living a lie and dragging an innocent child with me. I did not deserve Malikah. However, I loved her more than I loved anyone or anything. She was all I had, yet I had to give her up or else she would have been affected by my depression, her father's abuse of me, and the fact that the whole family was collapsing."

"Do you ever think that maybe leaving was not the right decision?" Lina asks.

"Every day," my mom replies. *"But God, I hope it* was *the right thing."* She has started crying now.

"Do you feel your depression is getting worse, or better?" Lina asks.

My mother laughs and says, "Definitely worse. I live all alone, I gave up my daughter because I felt she would be better off without me. I am incapable of having babies of my own, I gave up the one person who loved me despite all that. I am a lonely miserable woman," my mother says.

This first recording ends there. The second one is just a video of me taking my first steps and Mom coming towards me, lifting me from the ground and kissing me. My hair is brown, silky, and long. My eyes are hazel and my skin is olive tone. My mother's hair is curly and blonde. Her skin is white and fair. Her eyes are green. I try to imagine what it would have been like for my mother to wake up every day to a child she knew was not her own, pretending I that I *was* her own daughter—when we really don't have any resemblance at all. We look nothing alike in any way. I don't even look like Father. I look exactly like Lina. This must have been hard, not being able to have a child of your own but knowing when you adopt one that it's only fair this child eventually knows her real mother. Whatever it is she went through, I forgive her with all my heart. Because in the end, without her I would never have existed. Lina would have had an abortion and that would have been the end my life for good.

I wish I had known this sooner. I wish I was there with her, to heal her, and to help her. I hate that she lived all alone, I hate that she had depression and I wasn't there. I hate that she thought I would be better without her. Although maybe she had her own point. I don't know what was happening between her and Father, but I do know that I forgive her anyway. I am grateful she granted me life when no one else wanted me.

Chapter Twenty-Nine

My mother's house is nothing like ours. It's a definite masterpiece of art. It's all basic white color walls and HDF floors, but there are paintings literally everywhere. The furniture is all brightly colored, but matching together in a way that is so calming and beautiful to look at. I didn't know what my mother's profession was, but I found her business cards in her bedroom. She was an art curator, who apparently had her own art gallery right here in Soho. I suddenly remember Bilal's house and how cozy it is with lots of paintings on the wall. She must be the one who chose them for him. Her art gallery is called "Malikah." This surprised me for a moment, but made me smile. She has a photo of me in every room—her bedroom, the living room, and even the kitchen. It's sad how we never got the chance to talk. There are huge book-shelves containing art books, philosophy books, and probably millions of novels. I sit on her bed. It's so comfortable that I immediately fall asleep, waiting for Noah and Sarah.

I wake up to the sound of the doorbell and Sarah buzzing my phone which is vibrating right next to my ear. I rush to the door and open it for them.

"Oh God, finally! We were so worried about you," Sarah says as she hugs me.

"Welcome to my mystery mother's house."

"Wow," Noah says. "She was so artistic. This looks like a beautiful house."

"Yes, indeed! What did you say she did?"

"Art Curator." I give them my mother's business card. The both fall silent as they see the name of her gallery.

"So, what now?" Sarah asks.

"Now we go to my real mother."

"Let's move then," Noah says, putting down his bags. "Did Uncle Zayne call you?"

"He's tried to call loads of times, but I've blocked him."

Noah is speechless, but I can hear his surprise. Well, he has no idea how it feels to be me right now, so that's fine.

Lina's office is somewhere in Kingston. I just showed the taxi driver the address and he knew where to take us. London is cold but beautiful, no wonder Mom chose to flee here. We reach Lina's office building and all three of us stand in front of it. Each of us feels confused and scared in our own way. I am terrified to discover what this person is like. Whether or not I will regret coming here depends entirely on this moment. Noah is probably scared that I dragged him into this. Because, let's be honest, he is kind, loving, and always has my back but in the end it's really got nothing to do with him. Sarah, on the other hand is worried about me more than she is scared. She also feels awkward about the fact that the person we are about meet to is also her future mentor. She came here knowing that this will either end her scholarship, or make it even better. It's ironic how we all exist in the same place at the same moment, yet each one of us has completely different emotions towards what we are about to do.

I take a deep breath. I'm trying to go into this with an open mind, but all I can hear inside my mind is that this is the woman who left me behind. How can someone do that?

"Okay, I guess this is it," I say. "It's time to meet my other mystery mother." I laugh. I know it's not funny, but I am panicking. I'm trying to maintain a sane mind in my not-so-sane reality.

We enter the building and I search on the intercom for her name and find "Lina Morgan – Psychologist." I buzz the intercom.

"Why are you buzzing? We can just go in," Sarah asks. But I ignore her.

"Hello?" a woman's voice talks to us from the intercom.

"It's Malikah," I say. I hear the woman's breathing.

"I'm Mrs. Morgan's secretary. Come on up, we are on the second floor."

Mrs.? She is married! This is getting better. I wanted to write a novel and now my life is turning into one. How ironic is that?

We go up to the second floor and find a beautiful red-haired woman standing in front of the elevator. She is short and petite with freckles all over her face. She smiles at me and I sense the worry and yet curiosity behind her smile. My assumption is that she doesn't know the truth about me, only bits and pieces. My assumptions are nearly always right when they are related to emotions.

"Hello, Miss Malikah, nice to meet you. My name is Ruth."

"Hello, Ruth, nice to meet you too." I reply. She motions for us to go to the right, to an open door that is clearly an office.

"Does Lina know I am here?" I ask.

"No, I wanted to greet you first. I will tell her soon—but she is currently in a meeting."

This woman has no idea who I am but she knows my name, she knows I am important. I just don't know yet what else she knows. We enter a medium-sized office with two closed doors. I don't know which one is going to open up to reveal my biological mother, I can feel my heart pounding like I am running a marathon. I try to keep myself calm. This is just the zero step.

We sit down in the reception area and wait.

"Do you want anything to drink?" Ruth asks.

"No thank you. Please just tell Lina I am here. It's very important," I tell her.

"Alright, right away, don't worry. She just hates it when she is interrupted during an important meeting," Ruth says politely.

"Well, Ruth, this is more important than any meeting she's ever had," I tell her. I can feel my anger beginning to rise.

Sarah holds my hand and whispers, "You have got to keep yourself under some control."

I look at her in disagreement and frown. I know that she is right. However, right now, I have zero control. I hear Ruth whispering into the phone, obviously trying to tell Lina I am here. Suddenly one of the doors is thrown open, and a beautiful woman comes into the room. She has long brown silky hair, olive-colored skin, and wide hazel eyes that look worried and sleepy yet focused and intense.

She breathes deeply and stands still at the front of the room. The whole thing feels like a moment of epiphany or a slow-motion scene in a movie. She is wearing a high waisted black skirt and white shirt with opened buttons right above her breast line. She is wearing a simple gold necklace with a circle pendant. She has a few freckles on her cheeks, not so visible but I can see them. She has full lips just like mine. We look like copies of each other, and I don't know if that makes me angry or happy. At this point in my life, nothing makes me feel anything specific anymore. Her emotions are loud, heightened and clear. She is worried, scared—no, she is terrified. She has been waiting, anticipating, and preparing for this moment all her adult life and she is full of regret, pain, and love. She looks like a confident woman. A strong woman who knows exactly what she wants, yet twenty-one years ago she threw her child away. Ironically, she is now a psychologist who helps people become better versions of themselves. That's a joke for me, and yet I can't laugh now.

"Malikah," she whispers, but I hear her well enough. "Please, come on in." Her voice is musical and she sounds like someone who can sing. If I didn't know that she is my mother, that she is this terrible woman who threw me away years ago, I would have assumed she was such a beautiful human. But now, all I see is someone who abandoned me. And suddenly I feel like I no longer want to talk to her.

My heart is still pounding like I am running in a marathon. I feel pressure on my chest.

"I have to go," I whisper, running for the door. Sarah tries to run after me but Lina stops her.

In front of the elevator, I stand and try to breathe. I repeatedly press the elevator button. But just as it finally arrives, she stands in front of me and says, "You came all the way over here just to leave without speaking to me? Aren't you just a little bit curious?" She pauses. "You don't know me, but you've assumed lots of shit." I just stare at her apathetically. "You are possibly right, and I will let you go if you tell me just one thing. Why did you come here then?" she asks.

"Don't play therapist with me. You are a terrible person. So you better tell me your truth because I will know when you are lying. So please be aware of that, and be careful what you say," I tell her.

"You are right, I was indeed a terrible person. That was all in the past though." She sighs and continues speaking, "How do I make you feel now? If the voices tell you I am terrible, then okay I will let you go." She crosses her arms and makes her face completely neutral, giving nothing away. But I hear her emotions. She is desperate to hug me. She is desperate to know me, and I am making her feel hopeful in so many ways. I know she doesn't feel like a terrible person, but I had really wanted her to be bad, so that I wouldn't feel more pain for all the time we have missed out on. Pain from the fact that I never got the chance to know her, meet her, or actually be with her. I know this deep down inside of me, but I am not going to say it out loud. My heart's pace starts to slow, finally resting from the marathon.

"Okay, well played," I say. "My turn." I walk back towards the office, passing by Sarah's worry and Noah's anger. I enter Lina's office and sit down on a big leather couch in front of a huge comfy looking chair. Lina comes after me and closes the door. She sits in front of me and takes a deep breath. I stand up and take a tour around the room in silence. There are huge bookshelves housing many books about psychology, philosophy, cognitive behavior therapy, empathy, and neuroscience. She must be a genius. "Why?" I ask, not looking at her and trying to occupy myself with looking at the books.

"Why did I leave you?" she asks.

It hurts even more when she says it. I swallow and say, "Yes."

"I was a twenty-one-year-old orphan, with no money for her dreams. I came from a middle class family that had no ambition, unlike me," she paused. "All I had was ambition." She swallows. "And that made me selfish, made me determined to reach my goals." She sighs and I listen to her emotions, this story is causing her pain. "My mother died when I was five years old. I had literally no idea what being a mother was. My father, on the other hand, was a simple man who worked a nine to five job until he died just two years before I finished college. I had to live with my grandmother who was also dying, because she was pretty old. Although she was dying, she was a mean old lady who made me do everything around the house, like I was her slave. I had an English professor in college who liked how determined I was. She treated me like a daughter, but I treated her like a tool. Just another tool to help me get where I wanted to be." She pauses and I look at her.

"You are such a terrible person," I say.

"This is not the end of my story. You only have the right to judge me once I finish. So listen, Malikah."

I finally go back to the couch and sit down in front of her, but I hate how we are seated opposite each other. It feels wrong. Before I even say anything, she moves over to sit right beside me, saying, "You are not a patient. This must be very uncomfortable for you. It's better that I come sit next to you, if you don't mind?"

I am surprised by this, but I'm determined not to show this woman any emotion.

Lina takes a deep breath and continues with her story. Her English professor was very kind and loving to her. She was her mentor, and later helped her through the process of getting a full scholarship to come study her Master's in Psychology in London. This woman taught her empathy, kindness, and love, unlike everyone else in her life. Lina got pregnant with me when she was only twenty-one years old. She had just one more year until she finished college and her professor,

Elizabeth, helped her through. The same year she got pregnant with me, her grandmother was in the intensive care unit.

Linda was twenty-one and my father was twenty-six. She told me that when she got to know my father, he didn't even say that he was married. But she admits that it wouldn't have made a difference.

"I was toxic, drunk, and out of control," she says. "People assume a psychology major would be pretty focused and clear, but all my life really I had been a mess. I got into psychology because I loved learning it more than anything in the world." She lights up when she talks about her passion, just like we all do. My father and her were just having a fling—they both knew that. But when Mom found out about the pregnancy, she convinced Lina not to abort the baby. "She kept begging me and telling me that she believed this child would be her family's hope. She said she felt this really clearly. You were going to be the angel-sent baby that would make everything better. She offered me money, and selfishly I accepted it. But then when I got close to having you, I gave her the check back. I was only allowed to talk to her, not Zayne. That was Dahliah's condition." She worked hard to get through this phase. Her grandmother died and she had to stay with Dahliah in our house. Zayne wasn't allowed to be at the house unless my mom was there too. "Dahliah didn't trust him anymore, but she knew that she wanted you." Lina breaks into a smile. I see her tears, but she traps them inside and looks away, pretending that there is something in her eye. She takes a deep breath and continues. The world didn't keep her so apathetic and selfish. After she had me, she felt like something was slipping away. Like these two people were taking something that should have been hers. "I remember the day we were in the hospital and your father took your mother's ID to register her name instead of mine. That killed me," she says.

"What changed your feelings? You didn't want to have me anyway," I ask.

"Well, things changed. I changed. Everyone around me was so emotional, sympathetic, and helpful. My English professor believed in me, even though she realized I was using her. But instead of reacting to my selfishness, she treated me with her kindness and love. She knew I had no one, and she knew that its normal to be selfish and apathetic when you have never experienced love. She helped me grow in my education and I owe her that. She was such an icon. God rest her soul. Your mother… God, your mother was such a hero. She took me in, knowing I was the other woman, the one her husband cheated on her with. I agreed at first because, honestly, she was very nagging and I needed somewhere to live. But after that, after I got to know your mother and what drove her to keep this baby against all the odds, I felt more emotion than I had ever felt before. Your mother took care of me, and I knew deep down that she loved me like a friend. Your father was totally against the idea, but she convinced him anyway that this was the right thing to do. Who were we to kill an innocent baby? One who wasn't responsible for the mess we'd made in our lives?" she asks.

I laugh, "Well, she was right, but look at me now."

"The day it was time for me to go, the day my scholarship came through, I gave you to a woman who loved you more than she loved herself. I got a one-way ticket to London and as I boarded the plane, I suddenly started crying. I realized I had lost my child because I was selfish. I had been a terrible person, yet I was lucky to find kind-hearted people to help me. I felt like I didn't deserve their help. And at that time, I probably didn't."

"What about Adam?" I ask.

Lina smiles. "My best friend, Mariam, was one of the people I lost along the way because of how I was behaving. We only got back together after I flew to London and realized that I had lost my best friend. I am sure Adam has told you a bit about her? Before Mariam died she told me to take care of Adam, and I did everything I could to force his father to sign a waiver so I could be his guardian."

"Does that mean you adopted him?"

"No, dear that's not possible, I was just his guardian. I'm not his guardian anymore, since he passed the legal age years go. Plus, I am Christian and Mariam was Muslim," she says, smiling at me. "I know that will shock you too."

I am truly shocked, but I still show no sign of emotion and instead let her finish her story. "Well, Adam was like the hope that I lost when I gave you away. I treated him like my own. I read about the Islam religion so that I could bring him up the way Mariam would have wanted. After I had you, I discovered that I am incapable of having any other children."

"Why?" I ask.

"It just happened. God's plan, I think. I guess you were a miracle baby after all."

"So, let me get this clear. You left me because you were a selfish, manipulative, cheating, self-absorbed woman. But now are like the Goddess of kindness? Why the hell didn't you come back for me?" I ask angrily. She doesn't flinch.

She takes a deep breath and says, "Your father made sure that no one could take you away or even talk about what we had done. He made me and your mother sign loads of papers. We didn't really know what the papers were for. We trusted him, but we were stupid. I knew I signed an NDA but I didn't know what the other papers were. If I tried to come back for you before you came of age, I wouldn't even reach your doorstep. Malikah, it's bigger than any of us. Your father is not an easy person. He put restrictions around you like the fucking Great Wall of China. He became obsessed. Your mother told me that he kicked her out of the house because he believed she had no claim on you anymore. He wanted to raise you on his own, create that version of you that you know you really, truly, deeply hate. He didn't give us a chance, and your mother wasn't even allowed to have an opinion on anything. Then it got even worse when he discovered that his younger brother was actually in love with his wife. It was much more complicated." Lina has started to cry. "You were exactly what your mother said you would be. You were the hope for us all. But for this pregnancy—that in anyone's eyes would be called a mistake—I would have never turned out to be the person that I am today. I wouldn't have given Adam the life he needed, because I wouldn't have known what that was.

"Because of your existence, your mother was determined to pursue her dreams, and to make something of herself so that she could win you back when you reached the age of twenty-one. She hoped that she would be able to tell you everything and then you would be able to decide for yourself. Your poor mother couldn't handle it anymore, and I am sorry you had to witness what happened. We became friends when she came to me here in London, but I refused to treat her as a patient. She was the only person I could talk to when my own best friend committed suicide. And now another one has killed herself and it's like everyone around me keeps on dying.

"I am so sorry, darling, for everything that you have been through. I hope you find it inside yourself to forgive me. I know it is very hard. I wish I could go back in time, but well even that wouldn't change a thing. I believe that all of this happened for a reason. I would have never become the person that I am today, if I hadn't had an affair with a married man. You came from that relationship and then more and more I became a kind, loving, emphatic person. I became a person worthy of knowing and loving, unlike that old toxic and terrible version of myself. Malikah, you are a miracle. God knows how much I have waited for this moment."

She is crying heavily now and I don't know what to do. Her beautiful face is now red and her hair is messy. I reach for the tissues on her desk and hand them to her. She is genuinely honest and saying everything from the deepest darkest corners of her heart. I am guessing how much courage it took to tell the whole story without crying at every word. I try to imagine what it would be like to be Lina. I try to empathize with her and listen to her emotions. I try to put myself in her shoes, since that is what I do. And then I suddenly remember one thing my powers can do to fix all this.

I hold her hand and she looks at me through her tears. It's like I am looking in the mirror.

"You know I came here preparing for a fight, but you are so lucky that I can hear your emotions. I might not be able to forgive you right away—forgiveness takes time, even for empaths. But I can do this," I say, holding my hand up and putting it against her chest right on top of her heart. "Take a deep breath," I tell her and we both breathe in deeply. I see a light shining from my hands into her heart, and I take in all her pain. I take her worry, her self-resentment, and her regret. I feel all the things she has suffered, from apathy to isolation, to needing love. I take all of it away for this moment. And in my mind, I try to heal each emotion. When I remove my hand, it's like her face is shining. Her breathing is lighter and her tears have finally stopped. She looks at me in surprise and shock. She is lost words and yet she feels like she has so much to say.

"How do you do that?" she asks.
"I just do."

Chapter Thirty

How do you adjust to that? I mean how do you let all this information sink in, accept it, and move on? There is still so much that I don't know, and yet I am not sure that I want to know more. I am not sure if I can forgive her, and Father, and actually everyone who has caused me pain, lied to me, and controlled my life one way or another. People might think that because I am an empath I should have this magical power of forgiveness, but I don't. I don't know how to forgive this. I don't even know how to understand this. I left that day in Lina's office without saying goodbye. I just stood up after I healed her and I left. I went back to my mother's house with Noah and Sarah to rest and order some food. It took Noah a long time to figure out what to order, and how to do it. I lost my appetite the moment that woman started telling me her story and all I can think about is whether it's really possible for someone to turn from such a horrible and selfish person into this beautiful person I saw today? Does she deserve to be forgiven? What kind of papers did Father force them, trick them into signing? Too many questions have messed up my already chaotic mind. I don't know how to do this and for the first time in my life I feel like I want to go back the way things were. To be back at my father's office, pretending to be someone I am not. It's such cowardice I know, but at least then I knew what was real, what was not, and how to deal with it, at least on some level. Except of course for those times that I lost my temper.

Where I am now is just insane. My life is just not something anyone can relate to, or advise me about. Part of me still wants to shout so loud at her face and scream, "You abandoned me!" but then again, she was just a twenty-one-year-old woman with no family, no money, and apparently no soul. I can't sleep today. I can't eat either. I lie awake in my mother's bed, trying to let the tragedy that is my life sink in.

One more question fucks up my mind, did Adam know all of this all this time?

Apparently I did sleep in the end, but the next day I wake up feeling exhausted. Despite feeling so tired, I take a shower and get dressed. Noah and Sarah are still asleep in the next room, but I decide to go follow my mother's steps today. I found her notebook right on the nightstand beside her bed, all her appointments for today neatly planned out. I want to find answers to questions that I don't yet know. I just know that I should follow her steps, do the things she would have done today.

First, I go to her art gallery. It displays contemporary art pieces just like the ones at her home and at Bilal's. I haven't told anyone here who I am, but they seem to have noticed anyway.

"Are you Malikah?" a woman asks me as I admire a piece of art.

"Yes, do I know you?"

"No. But I know all about you!" She smiles and I feel her incredibly vibrant and energetic vibes. "I am Dee, your mother's trainer. I'm looking for her actually. It's been a few weeks since she came to her training, and her phone is switched off. I thought I'd come and check on her," she says. "I now know she must be occupied, because you are in town."

She clearly has no idea that my mother has died, so I break the news to her. "My mother is gone," I say, trying to maintain my stability.

"Gone?" she asks with a questioning expression on her face.

"Yes, she died a few weeks ago back in Cairo," I tell her and I feel my heart pounding and my chest getting heavy. *Please don't fall now, Malikah*, I beg myself.

This woman suddenly steps closer, "I am so sorry." And I see tears forming in eyes. "She was a beautiful human being. I wish you'd been here long enough to know her." She leans in and hugs me. This is the most awkward hug in my entire life, but I suddenly feel her energy and how calming it is, so I hug her back. I ease into it.

"Do you need anything? Does anyone here even know that she is gone?" she asks, still hugging me.

"No, I guess no one here knows," I reply. She breaks the hug and looks at me. "Then we must do something for her. Like a reception or a funeral at her house or something."

And suddenly this idea lights up my mind—this is one way to get to know my mother through the people who knew her. "That's actually a beautiful idea," I break into a smile. "Who did you say you are again? I am sorry."

"I am her pole and flexibility trainer," Dee replies, smiling again.

Pole? What the hell is that!! "Pole?" I ask in amazement. "My mother pole danced?"

"Yes, she was a great student too, so artistic. May god rest her soul." Taking out a piece of paper and a pen, she writes down her phone number, her name, and the name of her pole studio and hands the paper to me. "Think about hosting this funeral. I know a bit about your mother. I was her friend, as well as her trainer," she smiled. "And if you need anything, don't hesitate to call me."

She must know something about me. Her emotions are full of peace and gratitude. She looks like the type of person who loves people, something I can't relate to. So far everyone around me is either whispering about who and what I should be, or lying to me. I leave the gallery and wander the streets. I go to the restaurant where I know Mom was going to have her lunch. I walk past the pole studio "Dee's Pole Haven," then I see that at the end of end of her day today Mom was supposed to be meeting with Lina. But it doesn't seem like a therapy session—it seems like a dinner. I return to the apartment and find Noah and Sarah still trying to wake up.

"Morning, guys!"

"Where the hell were you?" Noah asks angrily.

"Out. I went through my mother's daily diary, and I followed her day—the one she would have lived today. She had nothing important on, though apparently she had dinner plans with Lina."

"When are we going back home?" Noah asks, cutting me off. He feels irritated.

"I am not going back home until I figure out what to do with what I know now," I tell him firmly.

"She has a point, Noah. Don't freak out just because your routine changed just a little bit," Sarah says.

Completely ignoring Sarah, Noah carries on, "Look, Malikah, this is all just insane. The day I told you not to be a coward and to follow your passion, I was talking about writing, not a mystery mother, and the truth behind your reality. I am exhausted, Malikah. We have to go back home to our normal lives. I can't answer my phone because you said we shouldn't let anyone know where we are, but I really need my life back, soon."

"I thought you were here to help me. To be there for me," I reply.

"I am, but I didn't know that you would leave us and walk around the city, or that you would demand more than just a meeting with Lina. I didn't know what to expect, but I am taking you home. This is all insanely unstable."

"You are not taking me anywhere, Noah. I am not your puppet. Don't treat me like all the other fucking men in my life. I am not twelve years old anymore. If you don't want to be here, then just leave, and stop whining about it. This insanely unstable life is my reality, thanks to Father and our great family ruining it for me. I now don't know how to deal with any of this. And you have no idea how I feel or how this affects me, so you either be there like you should or just leave me the fuck alone?"

Noah stares at me, speechless. I can feel that he suddenly realizes his selfishness. Sarah is also speechless and I feel their worry. Noah's selfish need to return home outweighs his concern for me and what I am going through. Sarah on the other hand wants nothing but for me to figure things out.

My phone rings. It's Lina. I leave leaving them both and enter my mother's room. When I finish the call, I tell them that Lina has invited us over for dinner.

"We'd better get dressed then!" Sarah smiles, trying to calm the tension in the room.

Lina lives in a vast beautiful house in Stanhope Mews East, South Kensington. Her house is probably one of the most amazing houses I have ever seen. Everything is one of four colors—white, beige, black, or gold.

She greets us at the door. A tall man with dark hair and blue eyes approaches us. "Hello, I am Tarek, Lina's lucky husband," he says, smiling. Tarek seems like a lovely man. He is a neurosurgeon and obviously has it all—the good looks, the money, and the genuine personality. Such a difficult combination. I try to find my way to the bathroom and I stumble upon Adam's room. I know it is his, even with the door closed, because I can hear his NF music playing loudly. I open his door to find him on the floor, doing push-ups. He stops and looks up, almost falling on his face when he sees it's me. He turns off the music and walks towards me.

"Malikah," he says. Why does he have to say my name so beautifully? I hate that.

"Adam."

"You are here."

"Yes, I am," I say without expression. "But I think it was a mistake."

I go to leave his room, but he grabs my hand and pulls me back.

"No, I am not letting you leave this time." I can feel his breath on my face. "You have got to believe that I didn't know all this time. I didn't know that you were Malikah, I didn't know shit, okay?" he says angrily, desperately trying to make me understand that he truly and genuinely did not know.

"But what did you do when you found out?" I ask.

He has nothing to say.

"Yes, that's what I thought. You are just a liar, Adam. Just like every other fucking person in my life. I mean, I am having dinner with a woman I just met who is supposed to be my mother. Nothing makes sense anyway. Nothing is going to make you any different. I am not here for you. I am here because I'm trying to figure shit out," I shout as anger soaks me from top to toe. Anger I have been trying to contain.

He steps back and says, "I wasn't sent all the way to Cairo to figure you out. I had no idea who you were. I knew the truth right around the time you knew—just a day or two after your mother's death. I didn't even tell Lina about you. Then she told me about Dahliah's suicide and that's when I discovered the links, and I had to tell her." He pauses and sits down on the edge of his bed. "By that time, I was already madly, deeply, and utterly in love with you. I didn't know how to say anything."

"It still broke my heart that you didn't say anything," I tell him.

"Well, Malikah, you aren't in my shoes, are you?"

"Well, Adam, you are not in mine either." I try to leave the room again, but he holds me back, pushing me against the wall so that we are face to face with our noses and foreheads touching.

"I am sorry," he says, and I see his tears. "I should have said something. I guess I don't like being wrong. But look at how life is now, it's insane, Malikah, and you are the only thing I am sure of." His eyes are crying but he tries so hard not to let it show. He leans in closer and gently kisses my lips. I kiss him back, but then push him away.

"I need to figure things out, Adam. I am sorry too," I tell him as I leave his room. I'm trying to calm down my intense, messed up emotions.

We sit down to dinner and Adam joins us. Noah and Sarah greet Adam with genuine love. Tarek tells us about Lina and Adam and about how they all created this little family out of nowhere. Tarek is divorced with two kids. He met Lina at a conference and he thinks of Adam like his third child. They share such beautiful stories. None of which I really understand as, in the end, I don't know what family feels like. As much as the stories are beautiful, they are breaking my heart a little bit more, knowing I never got the chance to feel all of this.

After dinner, Lina asks me to come by the treatment center later, to see what they do there.

"Look, Lina," I tell her. "This is not going to be a mother-daughter relationship. I barely know you and I will probably leave London after I find the answers I need to calm my demons down." I hear her emotions getting increasingly frustrated, but then they suddenly become hopeful.

"Well, you are here right now. Wouldn't one of your questions be to know what you can do with your powers? I mean you actually healed me in a strange way yesterday. It's like I felt safe, understood, and healed. This must be something else. Adam can't do that," she says. "You are special, Malikah. I guess you always have been."

"You don't know me. You know nothing about what I have been."

"That's true. But I know people; I am a psychologist." She smiles at me, trying to help me make sense of all of this. But I don't think anything will help me. "What do you have to lose? Just come by."

I don't reply, but I know that deep down inside of me I really want to visit the center.

"Have you discovered any other people like me and Adam?"

"No. So far we are keeping him a secret," she says.

"Why is that?"

"Well, we don't want other people treating him like a lab rat."

"Well, maybe you are not allowing him to reach his full potential?"

She is surprised. "I never thought about it like that."

"Thank you for dinner, but now we have to go." I walk towards Noah and Sarah to tell them we need to go, but she hits me with the million-dollar question.

"What do you want, Malikah?"

"Excuse me?" I ask.

"What do you want out of all of this? I mean, if you don't trust me, and you hate me and you are not willing to get to know me, then why are you here? What are the answers you need?"

"You lost your right to ask questions the day you abandoned me, MOTHER." I suddenly feel hate take over me. This is not who I am but I let it wash into me. I see her cry and feel her sadness and for some reason I just want to make her cry some more. Even though this is not what I do. I go to Noah and Sarah and tell them it's time to leave.

As we stand on the pavement trying to find a taxi, Adam comes running out to us.

"Let me give you a lift," he offers.

Sarah looks at me and it seems like she wants him to drive us. I roll my eyes and reluctantly get into his car.

We reach my mother's house. "Thanks," I say as I open the car door.

"You would love the treatment center," Adam says. "I know this is so hard, all of it. But this is your reality now, Malikah. You either deal with it or you don't. I understand you are angry. We all are one way or another. But don't take your anger out on the people who are desperately trying to make things work, who are desperate for your approval," he sighs. "This may not be the life you hoped for, but this is the life you are given. What are you going to do with it? Walk around hurting the people responsible, even as they are trying their best to be better? Or are you going to let all this sink in, no matter how insane and illogical it is, and find yourself all alone? It's your choice now. It's not your father's or your family's choice. I know this must be hard for you as since the day you were born you have decided none of this. You didn't ask for it but this is reality. What are you going to do about it?"

I look at him carefully and leave the car.

"I think this is where I leave you," I tell him as I close the door. I turn my back on him and walk toward my mother's house without looking back.

I don't know why I said that. But suddenly, my empathy and emotions turned apathetic. I thought I would be able to deal with all of this. I thought I would be able to accept it. I can't. This is not the life I hoped for, I understand that, but why does it have to be so damn hard? Noah is right. We should go back home. Maybe Father is a big madman liar, but he is the one who raised me. I think I owe him that.

Chapter Thirty-One

I sit waiting in anticipation for people to come to my mother's second funeral, the one I decided to host since no one in England knew that she is gone. I haven't told people how she died, I'm not ready to talk about it yet. So whenever anyone asks, I just start crying even when I don't feel like it. I am not ashamed that my mother chose to go this way, but it's just too hard to confess at this point.

Noah and I had another fight this morning, and he is still pretty mad at me. I told him again to leave if he wants to. I am not waiting for anybody to take care of me or lead my way.

"Stop being another version of all the other men in our family. Stop being like all the other men in the middle east!" I screamed in his face. He didn't like me saying that, but it didn't make me stop. I followed this sentence with "Daddy's boy." He broke almost all the plates we had on the dining table because he got so angry. I don't blame him, since the day I blocked my father and left the country to find out about my life, Noah has been pressured by me, my father, and his father, all three of us at the same time. But still, he has no right to claim himself an expert on what I am feeling or what I should do. I don't know why I have been so mean lately, but Noah hasn't been himself either. He has turned into someone who just wants things the way *he* wants, without any concern about anyone else.

"I didn't drag you all the way over here—you said you had my back," I shouted at him.

"I didn't know we would go around searching for your mother like a lost child," he screamed back at me. I knew he didn't mean it but it hurt anyway. I provoked him; I was mean too. Even though I didn't mean it either. I have come to the conclusion that when we are truly angry, when we say those things we don't mean, we secretly do mean them but are just too scared to admit it. I am not saying that this is always true, but fifty percent of the time I believe this to be the case.

"You did it!" Dee comes toward me, smiling.

"Well, yes, I think it's great to get to know the people who knew Mom," I say, smiling back. "Plus, look at all this food!"

"Honestly, kid, this is so beautiful of you. And you are handling it so well." Dee pauses to look at me for a moment and says, "I know she didn't raise you. I know the story. Not all the details of course, just bits and pieces. But from what I know, it's lovely of you to do this for her. She was a beautiful human. I wish you'd known her." Dee pauses and I can see tears in her eyes but she smiles anyway. "I am here for you, okay?" she says, hugging me tightly. This time, I don't feel awkward, since I know this is her way of showing love and caring. She is a hugger, I like that. Lina and Adam are here too, speaking to each other and to other people.

Adam comes to me and whispers, "This is so good of you." And smiles.

"Thank you." I look him in the eye. "I am honoring the one who kept me alive."

"And I am also honoring her because she is the reason behind everything," Adam says. I look at him in silence, just admiring his eyes. I try not to be too obvious, but I fail every time. Whenever I look at him time stands still. It's like we are the only ones in the room.

"I don't know if I can ever forgive you, Adam," I finally tell him and I watch as his expression changes. His smile fades and his cheeks flush red.

"Malikah, I swear to you that I knew nothing! Just like you. I fell in love with you because you are… well, you. I figured this all out after your mother's incident. I had no idea, Malikah please," he begs.

"But you still didn't tell me," I press my point.

"You were in the middle of a breakdown! How could I come to you and say, 'Hey, by the way, your mother is not your mother. Your real mother is actually my aunt. Actually, she isn't my aunt, she's the best friend of my dead mother. Oh and by the way, my mother committed suicide when I was twelve years old.' Can't you see it yet, Malikah?" he asks.

"See what?"

"That if none of this happened, you wouldn't have come here now. You wouldn't have had the courage to leave everything behind and follow your heart's burning desire to know more. This is where you will figure out more, and know more about yourself, Malikah. Not right under your father's feet. So if you ever feel like you owe your father anything, think again. Because you don't."

How did he even know I thought about that?

"I know how it feels. How all of it feels. What you are experiencing is like a mirror of my memories, I have been through worst phases than you can imagine. Focus, Malikah. Look around you. These people came for your mother. They all loved her and now they want to honor her. Would you have understood such a thing if you were still at home, scared? That woman over there, the one that you accuse of abandoning you, changed so much just because of your existence. I never knew that she'd had a baby, until she told me all about you. She never even showed me pictures. She looked at your pictures on her own. And when your mother came to her as a therapist, that was one poetic moment if you ask me. This life is well planned, no matter what we do. This is all happening for a reason. And if you can't be brave enough to face that reason then leave here and never come back. But if you were brave, you would actually confess your deepest truth. You haven't done that yet, Malikah. You haven't even confessed it to yourself.

"At the moment, you are walking around being mean to others. This is not you, and I know it's just a defense mechanism. Trust me, I have been there. But this will only be better if you talk about your truth, just as you tell others about their truths. So, ask yourself this, 'What is your truth? What version of you do you truly want? What are you going to do with the knowledge you have now?' The truth, Malikah, the truth you already know but are too scared to confess." He pauses and leans in to kiss me, but I avoid it.

"Well, I don't want to kiss you until I know my truth either."

"Fair enough," he says, and hugs me instead. "I know you'll figure it out eventually. Out of all the people in the room, I will always be the one who knows you best."

"What are you guys talking about?" Sarah asks, approaching us.

"I was just leaving, dear," Adam replies.

"Lina told me I should come check out the treatment center, since I am here. Obviously I am going to move here in few months anyway, for the scholarship. Do you want to come with me to the center?" Sarah asks me.

"Yes. Yes, actually I do," I reply, smiling.

Adam is right. I know my truth deep down inside of me. Out of all the people who know me, he will always be the one who understands me the best. Not only he is an empath just like me but he has had such similar life experiences. I look at Lina across the room and I find her looking back at me. She smiles at me and it feels like I am looking in the mirror at an older version of myself. I get nearer to her so I can listen to her emotions. She is worried, she feels love towards me. She is desperate for my affection and desperate to keep me here with her. She loves me so much but she knows she can't express it, because she realizes that I wouldn't respond well to her love. She is right, I wouldn't. I don't know her yet. But she has hope, so much hope inside of her, it's insane. I guess if someone has changed in a huge way like she has, she must have so much persistence and hope inside. No one is ever strong enough to fully change. And yet she has not a single drop of selfishness or apathy inside of her. Instead, she is empathetic, loving, and true.

"Thank you for inviting me," she smiles at me.

"You are welcome. After all, how many mothers does one girl have?" I joke and she smiles. "Did you invite Sarah to visit the treatment center just so I would go too?"

She rolls her eyes. "Well, maybe. Don't you want to go then?" she asks. I can feel that she wants to beg me, but understands that I need to choose for myself, which is kind of nice.

"I do actually. Adam told me all about it." I pause and then say, "I am sorry about yesterday. It's not my personality to make people cry. I am just—" I pause.

"—under a lot of pressure?" she carries on for me. "I understand it's not easy. There is no rush, but you have to know one thing."

"Yeah? What is that?" I ask.

"I will never let you go. Never again." She says this deeply, from the depths of her heart. I can feel her emotions screaming it too. I know she means it—I can feel she means it—and in a strange way it makes me feel safe, knowing there is this one person who will always be there. Someone who will accept me, even though I don't love or accept myself much right now. However true her emotions are, though, I will always doubt her. Not just because she abandoned me at birth, but also because no one in my life has been truthful so far. No one is what they seem anymore. My life is built upon a lie; I doubt anything and everyone. I doubt my emotions and my powers. I even doubt myself. It's hard to believe anything at this point, even if for a moment I know she is being truthful.

How can I have faith when I have lost faith in everything? And most of all I have lost faith in myself. In the end, I am nothing but a mistake. A human who wasn't meant to exist. And yet here I am, surrounded by people I don't know, mourning a mother I never knew, talking to the mother I should have known, leaving a lying manipulative father at home, whilst searching for the unknown.

"You matter to me. I couldn't do anything about it before, but since you know everything and are now past the legal age, nothing is stopping me from trying to reach you, Malikah. Even if you are so far away right now."

For a moment I feel strangely calm. It's like the calm I witnessed between Sarah and her mother a few months ago in the hospital; the calm and assurance that everyone dreams of feeling in their lives. I feel it right now, in this moment. I know it's new to me, and it's scary but instead of anger, I let the calmness soak me for once. And I breathe for the very first time since my mother's death.

Chapter Thirty-Two

The treatment center wasn't anything like how I imagined it. I assumed it would look and feel like a hospital. I thought it would be a sad place, full of depressed humans. But it isn't like that at all. For the patients, it feels like home. It feels like a safe place where they can come and talk about anything and everything, without fear of being judged, mistreated, or misunderstood. It is more like a house with comfortable vibes than a center for treatment. Strangely, the center makes me feel happy. Seeing all these broken hearted, depressed, abused, sad humans come here to feel better, be better, and to work for their mental health fills me with such strong emotions. The treatment center is on Marylebone Street. It's an elegant area but, well, so is the rest of London. From what I've seen, it's a beautiful city.

"I will be a part of this beautiful place soon," Sarah says. "You know it's pretty hard knowing what you want to do, I understand that. But when there is passion and drive eventually everything falls into place." She looks at me and smiles.

Sarah is so far the only person who has been right by my side even at my craziest moments. Noah is changing into the person that I believe has been trapped deep inside of him. He refused to join us today, he said he wouldn't feel comfortable and that we'd be better going on our own. He wasn't lying, I could hear his discomfort, but there is something else too that he's not telling me. However, at this point I have no energy to do anything or be anything for anyone so I accepted his decision not to join us.

We are sitting in the waiting area, waiting for Lina to come escort us.

"You know I finished my novel, and I have been editing it all this time?" I finally tell Sarah. Her face lights up and she hugs me tight.

"Oh my God, how? When? Oh God, this is amazing. Can I read it, please?" She is more excited than I have seen her in weeks. Sarah is usually pretty excited and wise and I love that about her.

"No, not yet. I am waiting for agents to reply to my query letters," I tell her. She breaks the hug and looks at me with her eyes wide.

"You even started sending out queries. Who are you?" She smiles.

"I guess I'm a pretty new version of myself. One who takes no more shit."

"That's my Malikah, embracing herself. I am so proud of you but I've still got to read it first, before anybody else. It's definitely a best friend privilege, everyone knows that!" She pouts. For the first time for so long, I feel light. I don't want to tell anyone else about my book. I only want to tell Sarah. She is the only one who so far hasn't lied or hurt me in anyway. Lina arrives and invites us to come with her. She greets me by shaking hands. She knows better than to try to hug me. She knows I will refuse her still.

We go through a door with the words "Group Therapy" on it. Inside the room I see Adam with a bunch of people who all look like they are probably in their twenties. Sarah and I sit far away from the group so no one will be made to feel uncomfortable by our presence. Lina joins Adam in the middle of the circle. The emotions of every individual are very high. But even though they are suffering deep down, being here makes them feel very calm. Adam is speaking about confessions and realizing your thoughts, about not being scared of them. This must be a new group, because most of the people seem a little bit nervous.

"Trust me, I feel what you are feeling," Adam tells them. "No one else knows this, but I am not just your doctor, I am also an empath."

"So what, I have empathy too," says one of the patients.

"No, I mean I have this power," Adam says. Then he goes to each individual in the circle, speaking the truth about each person's inner emotions. He is exposing them, but in a way which keeps them feeling safe. I didn't know Adam was a doctor. I knew he helps out, but I think he must be lying to them. I suppose it doesn't matter at this point, what matters is that he is helping them.

Each patient cries as Adam tells them what they truly feel. Everyone breaks down in their own way. One of them gets up to leave, but Adam stops him.

"You are here to heal and I am here to help. This is a safe place, trust me. Trust in this and I promise you, you are not alone. You are never alone." The patient's anger feels calmer and calmer. Sarah is right here, next to me, and she is stunned and amazed by what she is seeing. She feels so inspired.

"Does everyone know what you can do?" another patient asks Adam.

He smiles, "No, only the people who come here."

"That's a shame, you could help so many other people," the patient says.

"Well, I can't help anyone who doesn't want help, can I? But you guys are brave enough to come here, to speak, to realize everything deep within. You are here to heal and you have chosen this. I mean how many of you wouldn't have accepted this before?" The whole circle raises their hands.

"See?" Adam says. "People can be helped only when they too ask for it, when they realize that there is something wrong, or that they don't feel well. That's when they accept help. You can't help or try to heal someone by force, it has to be their choice. You can only raise awareness, and let humans choose what they want. The idea is not to rush yourself in the healing process, it's a process that takes time, that takes hard work. It's not easy to heal from within, but it *can* be done with your own will. Healing is not easy. Coming to therapy is not easy. I bet half of you wanted to leave before you even stepped through the door. But look at you, you made it. You made your first step. So, let's take it step by step, and have faith that we will heal, because this is a journey. Life is a journey and we have got to embrace ourselves along the way, with all our ups and downs and with all life's changes. That's just the way it is."

I suddenly feel ten times more respect for Adam, even though he hides things from me. I try to imagine what would have happened if he had told me sooner who he was, how I would have reacted. I would probably have screamed at him and called him a liar anyway. He wanted me to find it out for myself, and to lead this. He wanted me to choose to come here, to choose to run away, to choose myself for once. He knew that my mother's suicide would change me, although he didn't know which way I would go. He knew deep down that I would choose to know more about myself, and then I would have the ultimate choice. I finally understand.

It's the theory he uses with everyone, and especially with patients. He wants them to choose, to realize and to admit. He wants them to want to say the truth, to feel safe through the process, to feel like they *want* to heal, to understand that they are not being forced into anything. Using his empathy powers he helps even more, he keeps them safe and helps them realize that he has powers to know exactly what's deep inside and help them fix it. It's such a genius theory if you think about it. No one likes being forced into anything, especially someone like me who has been forced into everything—a major I don't like, a life I can't embrace' in fact, I've been forced into so many things, too many to count. I can't hear Adam's emotions, but as he finishes speaking he glances at me and I nod, assuring him that I understand, that I now know what he means. I may not have listened before, but I am listening now. I get it. And all I want to do now is go to him and kiss him so hard, and show him that I miss him more than anything. I want him to know that even in the middle of all my life's crazy insanity, I know I will never love anyone the way I love him.

In the end, though, the question remains, is that what I truly want? So, I love him, what's next? I haven't yet found what I am looking for. I have been searching for answers along the way. Love is not what I should be pursuing now, I need to find myself so that I can be able to love with a whole heart. I can't love, knowing I am not yet the person I should be, knowing I am not a whole person.

I am still trapped in this life, trying to figure out which way to go.

"He is seeming so genuine," Sarah finally says. "I feel like his words are coming straight from his heart."

"Yes, they are coming from his heart. He is an empath. Everything is coming from deep within." I turn to look at her. "I wish I could go there and heal those people for just a moment."

"Why don't you?"

"I guess it's not my place to do that."

"No, Malikah, you should go. What's stopping you now? This is who you are. You were born for this," she says, but I don't answer. The session ends and Adam comes over to us.

"So, what do you think?"

"I think I didn't know you were a doctor," I smile at him.

"Well, I'm still in the process of finishing my degree. I told you I also read a lot."

"Was that speech aimed at me? Am I a patient now?" I ask him.

"Malikah, love, we are all patients one way or another. Sometimes I give a speech that is also for me. I heal with them."

It has been so long since I heard him call me love. Has it been a long time? Or is it just that the days feels like years now? I have been trapped inside myself for so long. We are all patients, that's true, we are all broken one way or another deep inside. No one goes through this life and stays completely whole. Some people change for the better and some just let the worst side of themselves take control.

"So, what will it be for you? How are you planning to heal?" Adam asks.

I hug him tight and he hugs me back. I smell his scent. It feels like I'm home again. I feel him smell my hair as he buries his face in my neck.

"God, I have missed you," he whispers.

"I have missed you too, but I'm not sure this means anything right now." I pull away from him. "You know I haven't figured out what I am going to do with Father, or with all the facts and truths I have learned so far." I take a deep breath and continue, saying, "Adam, I love you. I have never and will never love anyone as much as I love you. But I can't be anything or anyone until I find my true self among all this chaos." His expression doesn't change. He is still smiling and still standing there listening to me.

"I am in awe, Malikah. I am truly proud of you and I know you don't feel it yet or you don't know it yet but this is the truest you have ever been. You are choosing to find your Self. You didn't choose to please me, or be passive. This is what you need to do. I will be here. Waiting like an old man waiting for his lover to come back. I know you will come back to me. This love is just too epic for us to let it go." He smiles into my eyes and pulls me in to hug him again. "You have got to know that I never lied to you. I never knew anything." I pat him very gently on his back to assure him.

"You don't have to explain now. I think I understand."

We finally let go and look at each other smiling. I search for Sarah and she is right there laughing and talking with Lina.

"How do you feel?" Adam asks.

"Toward Lina?" I ask and he nods.

"I don't feel anything yet. It's so weird and uncomfortable. It's all too much, Adam. It's just so hard."

He looks at me with his sparkling walnut eyes and says, "I understand."

"I still have so much confrontation to do."

"Well, take all the time you need to process this, until you reach where you plan to be. Hopefully that will be right in my bed, where I can wake up next to you every morning. But you know it has to be what *you* want, what *you* choose."

I laugh, "God, why did you have to be so beautiful?"

He smiles and I feel so calm. Then Lina comes and breaks the moment saying, "So, what do you think, Malikah?"

"It's great, what you guys do here," I say, trying to sound like I'm a normal person talking, but it's just so hard to be normal around her.

"I would love it if you let me do some tests to figure out more about your power," Lina says. But Adam looked at her in disagreement.

"Excuse me?" I frown at her. "I am not here to be your lab rat."

"No, Malikah don't misunderstand me, I tested Adam so we could know more about his strength, nothing more. It's a way for you to understand yourself. Don't you want that?" she asks and I know if I listen closely to her emotions I will understand, but I choose not to listen.

"Well, Lina, I am still not your lab rat. And this is not the way to get closer to me if that's what you intended," I say angrily. "I think we have to leave now." I walk away and motion for Sarah to come with me.

Sarah follows me to the taxi and, on the way home she finally says, "I don't think that's what Lina intended, Malikah."

"I know," I answer without looking at her.

"You know? Then why did you act so aggressively?"

I remain quiet but she nods her head. I know she understands. I can't accept this Lina person, no matter how great she is, how perfect she is. It's just hard for me to accept her. I try and try, but it just doesn't feel like I can do it. I don't know how to react to her except either aggressively or with no expression at all. Even though I know through her emotions that she means everything she says and does. I can't accept her. Every time she opens her mouth, all I hear in my head is that this person abandoned me.

"I think I want to go back home," I say eventually. Sarah looks at me and nods without saying a word.

She holds my hand. "It's hard, I understand that. But among all this madness, I am still here, okay?"

"That's the thing, I don't want anyone here, Sarah. I want to figure this out on my own. I think I want to go back and talk to my father, maybe apologize to him for being such a fuck up daughter. I don't know if this is the right thing to do, but I think I need to try."

"Apologize?" she says, dropping my hand. "Malikah, this man is the reason for all of this, why in hell would you apologize?"

"He stayed, when no one else did."

"No, Malikah, he forced them all to leave. Can't you see it?" Sarah says.

I don't look back at her, I just say, "I think we should go back home." And deep down I know, at this moment I have no home.

Chapter Thirty-Three

Noah hasn't been answering our calls all day and when we get back we find that he has packed all our stuff and bought three tickets to Cairo. Sarah is so close to losing her temper with him. She can't believe he wants to leave so badly that he doesn't even care how the rest of us feel.

"You know that I have to come back here soon, right?" she says.

"Yes, but then we'll have a plan. We won't be living in some stranger's home, doing things we don't get," Noah says. The room falls silent. I look at him in shock.

"You know, Noah, sometimes you are a pure asshole, and if it wasn't for this trip, I wouldn't have known," Sarah says bitterly and leaves the room.

I have already decided that I will go back to Cairo, but not because of Noah. I'm going to get some kind of closure with Father, if he even accepts me back. I now know I can't decide anything for myself in life unless I say what I have to say, and do what I have to do to feel better. So, I think to myself, why not tell Noah that he has turned out to be just like our parents intended. That he has been panicking simply because this is not how he expected his day to go, that he doesn't care at all about how everyone around him is feeling. I know he feels ashamed deep down and sorry for me but I don't need people to feel sorry for me. Especially not Noah. I want him to understand that all of this is just way harder for me than it is for him. In the end I tell him, "You turned out to be everything you criticized. Isn't that ironic?"

"Excuse me?" Noah splutters back, in confusion.

"I mean, you used to walk around talking shit about our family and how they expect you to be a certain type of person.

But look at you; you turned out to be just like them. You are not over-protective, you are controlling. You are not feeling uncomfortable, you just hate that things aren't going your way or to your plan. I irritate you because you know you can't control me, and you know that I could explode at any second. I just want you to understand something. I don't want you to take care of me or be my father, I have had enough of this fakeness. I just want you to be true with me. If you want to leave, then leave. I have been telling you this since we got here. At first, I thought you were Noah, my cousin and my friend who just wants to stick by me. But it's not like that deep inside of you, is it? I irritate you and mess up your life with my insane, unstable, unreliable life. Well, guess what, Noah? I am fucking trying my best to make sense of it too. I am not coming back to Cairo because you are forcing me. You are in luck that I have already decided to go back. So when I've decided which place to choose, which version of me I want to be, it will be me—Malikah—who chooses. And no one else. And I promise you, once I have decided, you will never see my face again."

"Do you really think your father will take you back, Malikah? You literally tried to burn the house down, then you stole his money and then you ran the fuck away to goddamn London to find your so-called mystery mother. Why do you even care about her? She abandoned you anyway? I think you are searching in the wrong places," Noah shouts.

"You know what?" I spit back at him. "You are just like everyone else. You will never understand. I thought you would, but I was absolutely wrong. Let's go back to your fancy penthouse and your sure, certain life. But when we do, don't you dare come running for me, asking for shit."

I guess people change, according to the conditions they are going through. Sometimes they change for the best, sometimes they change for the absolute worst, and some people realize who they really are only by change. Noah is a sweet guy but all of this has brought out all his true beliefs, and all the things he was raised to believe in. Now he is slowly turning into my father and Jabril. In the end, in anyone's eyes he is just a man, a middle eastern man who wants to take control. A man who doesn't like it when a woman leads. A man who doesn't like it when a woman just leaves in pursuit of who she is. He is still such a beautiful person in so many ways, just not so beautiful with me anymore. For him now, I am just another woman out of control.

When we land in Cairo, it feels like the warmth of home. I haven't said it, but I've missed this place more than anything. I smile uncontrollably at the beautiful feeling of coming home but I soon remember that this place rejected me so much more than it ever accepted me.

Noah gets his own taxi; he doesn't want to be in the same car as me. The car looks awful. No one has looked after it in the two weeks we have been away. Sarah gets into the car with me and I drive her home. She has just broken up with Noah, on our way back here on the plane. She simply can't stand the side of him that has finally appeared. Sarah is the type of person who knows what she wants, and Noah isn't it. I wish I could be more like her.

"You will be careful," she demands.

"Yes," I lie. I actually have no idea what I am going to do.

"If anything happens—" she starts, but I cut her off.

"I will call you, Sarah, I promise. Please just take care of yourself, go upstairs to your mother and be the perfect daughter. Don't worry about me. I want you to be OK too. You just broke up with the man that you thought was the love of your life." I hold her hands to reassure her. "I love you, Sarah, and I know you care so much about me, but I have got to do this on my own." I break into a smile but I can't help but tear up. I don't know if I can go back to the penthouse or what will happen if I do.

"Okay, I love you. Always remember that," Sarah says. "I am going back to London soon if you want to go back. I just have to know where to settle, so that I can start my masters next month."

"I don't know if will go back," I tell her. "I have so much healing to do from within."

"Okay then, just take care." She leaves my car and I watch her walk away, back to her warm home and the mother she loves so much. Noah has also returned to his penthouse and the people he belongs to.

I drive the streets, not knowing where to go or how to confront my father. I want to talk to him and apologize for my behavior but I also want to scream at his face and break the whole house on his head. But then I realize what I really want to do. I really want to see Bilal.

I call his mobile to check if he's home. He doesn't pick up at first, but I keep calling and he eventually he picks up. He tells me that he has moved, and has taken a house in Dokki all by himself so I drive to him.

The house he is living in is right in front of the shooting club, on the top floor. He can see most of the city of Cairo from up here. Bilal opens the door wearing just his boxers and a rope. He holds a bottle of black label whisky in one hand and a pack of cigarettes in the other.

"What the hell are you doing?" I ask.

"Drowning my sorrows." He is smiling. But it isn't a genuine smile. He is broken and hurt. His face shows the extreme pain that only a sarcastic smile can express.

"Did you think it would all be okay when you left the penthouse? Your father went fucking crazy," Bilal says as he lights up a cigarette. "You want some whisky?"

I frown and say, "No, thank you. Tell me what happened."

He stumbles to the couch and lets himself fall down on it. "Well, he was screaming at all of us. Running away, stealing his money, and burning your clothes in front of him was not an easy thing for him to deal with, Malikah. He is a father at the end of the day, no matter how bad he seems." There is an awkward silence. He is lying, why is he lying?

He bursts out laughing at his own words. He is so drunk and unstable.

"I am joking! That bastard deserves all the shit coming his way," Bilal says, laughing. I sit and watch him crumble. He is falling into a depressed, sad version of himself and I can't help but ask about my mother.

"Tell me about her?"

His eyes open wide. He sits up and takes a deep breathe. "Oh, Malikah, she was my angel. Of course, I didn't get to make her mine or give her my entire world, but God knows this woman has my heart till the day I die." He pauses and says, "Which is soon apparently."

He is laughing again, but I don't twitch.

"I am sorry, it's just—" he pauses and I can feel his pain. Oh God I can feel his pain. I want to sit here and drink away my sorrows with him. But I can't do that, and I can't let him break himself apart either.

"Your father used to love her, and she loved him too. But when our father, your grandfather, died, your father had to be in charge of everything. When he became the head of the entire empire, oh that changed him into who he is. He wanted people to follow his command, obey his rules. He wanted to be and do whatever he pleased. I understood that all too soon. The same thing happened with Jabril. But, well, your father was always the alpha and the alpha rules all." He takes a sip from his drink and stubs out his dying cigarette. "Dahliah saw what was happening and came to me to talk. She had no particular intentions, but I was there for her. Honestly I fell for her, way before she ever fell for me because let's be honest, how could I not love her?" Tears are streaming from his eyes but he doesn't stop. "You know the logo of my company?" he asks me.

"No?"

He takes out his phone and shows me his wallpaper. "A flower?" I ask.

"Not just any flower, it's the Dahlia flower," he says. "Your father was so mad when I left the company to pursue my dream of being an interior designer, my dream to create my own manufacturing company. But I did it anyway. Want to know why?"

"Why?"

"Because your mother motivated me to do it. She was the fire in my soul and although I never got the chance to give her the love she deserved, I know she knew how I felt." He took another sip of his whisky. "Your father beat me up when he knew. He nearly gave me concussion. But I let him beat me. I knew it wasn't easy for him to realize that she didn't love him. Not because he loved her, but because he felt she was his own property. For her to love his own brother, or more precisely for his own brother to fall madly in love with his wife, that wasn't easy for him. I let him beat me until I bled. But you know when I got up off the floor, I knew she would still love me and I would still love her anyway. We never acted on that love, for sure, but God I knew how she felt."

"Why did she leave?" I ask.

"Oh, dear Malikah, everything was messed up. Your father beat her up more times than I can remember, way before he even knew about our affair. He just likes being in control. Plus she stopped having sex with him, when he started cheating on her with every woman in the fucking country. Then she started confessing her true emotions about not loving him. He tried taking you away from her so many times when you were younger, but she always held on to you. She was always submissive to him because she wanted to be there for you. But then she realized that she was not going to be good for you, that her depression was causing problems. She planned everything. I knew that leaving wasn't going to make her any better, but she left because she had to, or else you would have hated her too. Or maybe you would have killed yourself." He is still crying. "She didn't leave because she wanted to leave. Your father forced her to leave. Not only by abusing her, but by forcing her to sign papers and many, many other things. If she hadn't left when she did, she would have probably died sooner." He refills his whisky glass and now I start to cry too.

"Your father didn't use to be like that, Malikah. But oh dear his hunger for money and power was just inevitable." He smiles at me through his tears. "He wanted you to be just like him. But look, he has failed miserably. He thought if he eliminated your mothers, then he would have full control over you but, oh boy you failed him miserably. And therefore, his plans failed too."

"What do you think I should do?"

"Find your closure. Talk to him. Maybe that will help you to find where you truly belong. Since this is a lifelong journey, I am telling you from the other side of life, be who you want to be, dear, because life is not worth it if you aren't." He throws back the whisky in one shot, and then brings the bottle to his mouth.

I take the bottle from him and ask, "Have you been drinking for the whole two weeks?" I hold the bottle away from him as he reaches out.

"Yup, three meals a day is now three times the whisky." He laughs a drunk laugh. "Oh I think I am sick. Did I have too much whisky?" he laughs. But then he throws up on the floor.

"We have to get you to a hospital," I tell him, trying to hold him up. I call for an ambulance and wait beside him.

At the hospital emergency room, I wait for him outside. The doctor has told me that the level of toxicity in his blood is very high and that he needs to stay at the hospital overnight. I return to his home and pack him some clothes.

Chapter Thirty-Four

I have been sleeping on the couch since yesterday, my back hurts but my head hurts even more. Bilal has finally woken up, and he is sober. But he is still in pain. It's a shame that alcohol can't take the pain away. Adam and Lina have been calling me, but I've turned off my phone. I don't want anyone to distract my thoughts right now. I don't want any good or a bad influence. Instead, I want desperately to hear my own thoughts, and to understand my own mind.

"Good morning," I say to Bilal, who is still trying to open his eyes.

"Morning, yes. Good? I don't think so," he says and I can't help but laugh. How can he joke, even now?

"Well, morning then," I say.

"Much better," he says, smiling. "Thank you."

"What for?" I ask.

"Saving me. I would have probably died from the amount of alcohol that was in my body, but you came just in time," he smiles at me and I feel his gratitude. This man is too genuine for this world.

"Well, you don't need to thank me," I smile back.

"What have you been doing? Why are you up this early?" he asks.

"Writing."

"Can you read me some of what you wrote?"

"It's a poem," I pause. "I woke up not feeling good. But I haven't been feeling good anyway, so I decided to write a poem about being lost."

"Oh, that's my type of poem. Read it for me, if you don't mind?" He looks weak and pale and is clearly still in pain. But he still wants to talk, laugh, smile, and be there for me.

"Okay," I say, smiling as I hold up my phone to read what I just wrote. "It's called *Too Many Versions*."

"Okay, I am all ears."

"There are so many different versions of myself.
It's hard to know which one is the real one anymore.
There are so many, I have lost count…
There is the passive and the pleaser.
There is the lover and the cheater.
There is the kind and the caring.
There is the hated and the hater.
There is the angry and the insecure.

There is actually no cure,
For what I have is nothing pure.
It's not about being mature.
You see, I am very unsure
What version of those I must endure.
What version I must secure.
What version should take a detour.

What I know for sure is that
I will never be any of these.
I am not anything anymore.
I am merely a body with no definite soul.
I am just a person with no road to crawl,
Just intersected, messed up, neglected, imperfect, mentally ill, and dejected roads inside my mind.

An outcast, a misfit, a loner you see.
You can't fully grasp every part of me,
For I am a mystery even for my own self.
My mind is a maze I am lost in.
It has monsters and ghosts from my own creations.
A fiction writer, I am my own domination.

My mind is not a normal brain.
It's abomination.

I'd rather sit in my room; I prefer alienation.
I'll calm my demons and do my own filtration.
Just let me be, let me for once, please
Embrace my own sensations…"

Bilal looks at me in amazement. And finally says, "This is beautiful, Malikah, I felt it so deeply. I know it's not possible, but in so many ways you remind me of your mother, not the biological one but Dahliah. She would have cried, hearing your poems."

"I love that you know so much about her," I break into a smile. "Even though it hurts me that I have no idea who she was."

"Well, look at it this way. She was just like you, only with blonde hair." He smiles and I can't help but laugh at his comments. Not because it's comedy, but because he is so passionate even in his down times. He is sad with passion, he loves with passion, he cries with passion, and even when he is sick, his passion for everything is still there.

The doctor arrives and breaks into our conversation. He wants to run some tests. Yesterday they were inserting tubes into Bilal's mouth to help him breathe and today he is talking about the love of his life; his passions. What a combination of thoughts. We sit and wait for the test results. I tell him all about the letter and the flash drive. I tell him why I burned the clothes that father bought me, about how "I was trying to make a statement."

I was defensive, even though Bilal didn't disagree with anything I said.

"You stole from the man. But still, you are his daughter," Bilal says. "However, I am not sad for him. He deserved everything he got. But you know that his natural reaction to all of this is just to freak out."

"Why did you move house?" I ask, and his expression changes.

"Well, for starters, your father thought I made you do all this. Then he told me I didn't deserve to live in the family home, since I am no longer part of the family, so—" Bilal stops.

"He packed your clothes in trash bags just like he did with mother?" I ask, and Bilal nods.

"I went back for the rest of my stuff later. I should have moved anyway. So, I stayed at a hotel for a while until I found this lovely apartment. It's ten times bigger and better, although I am sad I don't wake up by the Nile every day," he says, smiling.

"What will he do if he sees me then?" I ask.

"You are his daughter. I think the worst thing he can do is shout at you," Bilal says, but he is lying. He knows Father is capable of more than that. He sighs and says, "Or, I don't know, your father might surprise me but well, in the end, there is nothing more precious than a daughter, right?"

"Well, at this point I have no idea, Bilal."

"What are you really trying to do here?" he asks. "Malikah, are you trying to get closure from your dad? Or are you trying to forgive him? Or are you trying to seek forgiveness? Or what?"

"No, I am not trying to seek forgiveness. I did nothing to be forgiven for. He is the one who should seek forgiveness."

"Well, your father isn't capable of saying that he is sorry."

"I know," I answer immediately.

"So now what?"

"I just want to talk to him. I want to tell him I know everything now. I want to hear what he has to say for himself."

"Then what? Hug and make up?" Bilal asks sarcastically and now I am getting irritated. "I am sorry, Malikah, but that is not how it's going to be. I wish it was different, but if you're going to your father then you should prepare an apology, because he will want to hear you say you're sorry, before he will talk about anything else."

"But I didn't do anything!"

"No, Malikah. For him that isn't true. You ran away and stole money from his bank account." Bilal says, "I am not defending him. I am just telling you his perspective."

The conversation ends abruptly as the doctor arrives to tell Bilal that he's good to go. All I am feeling now is guilt, because Bilal is right, I *did* run away. But my father has lied to me all my life, so why should I be the one to apologize? Now, before I can talk to him I have to apologize? And then hope that he will properly talk to me? Oh, dear Father, you have caused me enough pain already.

"What day is it today?" I ask.

"You're asking a person who just toxified himself with alcohol?" Bilal says sarcastically. "But it's Tuesday, why?"

"You want to see a side of me that I don't show to everyone?" I ask.

"Always!"

I take him with me to the Art Café open mic night. I've given him clear instructions about not saying my name, and told him that he has to call me "The Poet."

It has been so long since I came here that everyone is coming over to say hello.

Feeling like a movie star, I go up on stage. With the crowd's eyes on me, I feel nervous but it feels like home; it feels normal. Just like the life I had before I ran away. I never thought I would miss that life, but here I am missing it.

"This poem is about emptiness. The feeling you get when you are lost, the feeling of having no home, nowhere to belong. And there is nothing you can do about it. This poem is about a feeling that is not foreign to any of us. This is about the darkness life has put me through, leaving me hollow and with no clue what to do next," I pause and smile at Bilal, who is sitting right in front of the stage. I wrote this poem not so long ago. It comes from the deepest corners of my heart, where I found my tears escaping with no boundaries and nothing to hold them back.

"Emptiness is no foreign feeling.
I have felt it many times throughout my life.
Usually, it's when the darkness
Finally, takes over the light.
Emptiness is no foreign feeling.
I have known it since I was a child.
It has been living deep down
In a hollow hole inside.

Emptiness is no foreign feeling.
Do you think I am exaggerating?
I know when I feel it.
I am out of feelings again.

Emptiness is no foreign feeling.
I feel it creeping in,
Swallowing my heart and emotions.
I gave everything,
But nothing seems enough.
Let us mourn my dead emotions and lock them deep inside.

I am made out of piles and piles of
Unsaid emotions,
Mistreated actions,
Unaccepted and ignored
Confusions.

Emptiness is no friend of mine.
It comes once in a while.
I have poured my heart out,
And cracked my brain open.
I am not a foreigner to emptiness,
But I hate how it feels.
Anger consumes me,
That's the only thing I feel.
All my emotions have been rejected
By me, by you, by them, by the world.
Emotions are rejected everywhere.

Everyday.
Emptiness is my prison.
A prison with no escape.
Goodbye freedom,
I never had you anyway."

As I finish the crowd claps and Bilal stands up to hug me. He feels proud and he feels love and among all his pain he still has a gratitude and passion for life. If he could be completely healed, he would embrace this even more. I let my tears flow; I don't hold them back anymore. I would rather cry my heart out now, because that's the only way to express the exact way I am feeling.

Bilal and I walk around el Zamalek and I tell him about my powers. I tell him about the time I healed my mother. I tell him that as a child, without any idea what was happening, I knew from within me that I wanted her to feel peaceful and better for a moment.

"I don't know how long it lasts. But I guess it makes the person feel more understood and calmer," I say.

"Can you heal me? I want to know how it feels," Bilal asks.

I tell him about my powers and all the things I have known and discovered so far, but he doesn't freak out or even seem surprised. It's like he already knew, deep down, that I am no ordinary person.

"Of course, I can heal you." We get into the car and look at each other. I was in the driving seat, and he was sitting next to me. I press my hand on his chest and I ask him to breathe. We synchronize our breathing and I close my eyes. A light emerge from my hand, and shines into his chest. I felt my light wash his insides for a moment. He closes his eyes to embrace the moment and take the light into himself. For a moment everything feels so peaceful. As the light returns to me, I raise my hand and we both breathe deeply.

"How do you feel?" I ask. "I never know how others feel."

Bilal looks at me with a tear in his eyes and I recognize it as a happy tear.

"I feel like all my wounds have been healed. Not entirely but it feels like you gave me assurance, love, and safety all at once. I feel like I know that things are going to be better. It's like you absorbed all the pain and turned it into a belief that life is going to be better. I feel like a newborn man, waiting for the next step in life." Bilal takes a deep breath, inhales and exhales, feeling the air in his lungs so deeply. "I feel like I can breathe. Malikah, this is a gift. I can't believe you don't really use it. I mean you are basically a Goddess!"

I smile but don't know how to reply. Then he says, "I am not kidding, this is a miracle. Does this Adam guy do the same?"

"No," I reply. "But he kind of knows how to read minds."

"This is unbelievable!" Bilal exclaims. "You are a Goddess." He pauses and then says, "Goddess of emotions, healing, and passion." He says it loudly and passionately and I almost believe it, but instead I laugh.

"Don't push it. It's a gift but I am no Goddess."

Bilal looks at me and pouts, "Oh, okay, Miss Humble Goddess."

After the open mic night, I drop Bilal off at his house. Before he leaves the car, he says, "You should embrace who you are, no matter what happens. No matter how much the world around you rejects you. You will find yourself only in your passion, Malikah. Remember that. I can't wait for you to write a book or something. You have so many talents, kid. Remember that. And your Uncle Bilal is always here for you." He hugs me and says, "Thank you for healing me."

I know deep down that the next step is not going to be easy, but it's good to take this step. I will talk to my father, I will call him Dad, I will have my closure with him and give him the healing he too so badly needs. I will apologize for hurting him because no one wants to be abandoned by his child. And although I feel this task to be so heavy, I will try to be a good person, because this is who I am and this is who I should embrace. He will take me back, after all I am his daughter. And maybe then I will find my closure and convince him that Lina should be in my life. Maybe he will see that things will get better, if we can only learn to communicate. Life is going to get better, it's not the end of the world. It never is. Healing Bilal today gave me so much energy to face my fears. What's my ultimate fear? Confession. What's my ultimate goal? Closure. Who is the ultimate cause of my pain? My father. But I will fix this, I tell myself. *I will fix this*. Maybe I can make it all better.

Chapter Thirty-Five

Confrontation isn't my best talent. I will literally do anything to avoid it. Saying out loud what I feel really scares me, and so far, I am not very good at it. But talking to my father is something I have got to do. I know that he's the reason behind everything, but I do believe that there must be an explanation. And if there is no explanation, I just want to make up with him and then leave to go my own way.

I am still waiting for an agent to accept my book. So far all I have had is rejections. I don't even know if I can do it or not, if I can be a writer. But here I am, waiting for just one acceptance message from the 200 queries I sent out. Maybe being a writer will change my father's mind. Maybe achieving my dream, the one he used to mock and belittle, will help him see another side; a side that is not his for a change. Well, these are all just hopes and dreams. Right now, my knees are weak, I haven't slept all that much and my brain is going to explode from overthinking. It's like I am suffocating. I have been staying at Bilal's house for a week now, helping him to avoid the drink, but also trying to find the courage to apologize to my father, to explain why I ran away. All I know is that I want to embrace who I am, and if an empath should be forgiving and brave enough to let go, then I want my father to be the first person I heal. I want to travel the world and learn more and more about writing. I want to really pursue my dreams. I want to heal people and be with Adam. I want so badly to freely embrace who I am, with no one to set limits on what I can become. I want to be remembered; I want to be the hero of this story. So far everyone else has been writing my life for me, everyone has been forcing their opinions and perspectives on me. I have been following their tracks, and trying so hard to leave my comfort zone, to see the truth and to make my own decision. I have been influenced by others and I don't want to be like that anymore. I just want to be who I am. And I might not know who that exactly is right now, but I am trying to figure it out.

I am trying to take bits and pieces from all the trauma, pain, lies, and manipulation I have so far experienced, to create something good in me. I have been fighting with myself every day, losing control. But it's not because I am crazy, it's because I feel heavy. I feel heavy every day. I lose my temper and do crazy impulsive things because it's all too much for me to handle. It's all just too much for me to feel. I find it hard to accept that my powers are not a curse, to believe that they are a gift, but then I find others refusing them, getting scared of them. I feel sometimes that I should lead a life of loneliness, so that I can achieve what I believe is true in my own way.

All I want to do is scream. Scream about the reality that I have witnessed, expose my powers to the world, take who ever accepts me and be there for them. I have been passive and in denial. I have become everything I have criticized, and it is scaring me. I can't be like that. I need to let go, to forgive, to try my best to forget. I need to be the person I am supposed to be, the best version of who I am. And to be that, I have to face that one fear I have been ignoring my whole life, to say all the words I have been denying, suppressing, and keeping inside.

I feel like I might explode with anger. I'm trying to control it, but I can't deny my anger anymore. I was doing what I thought was good; being the good daughter and the good friend. But then I realized that I don't have to deny everything that I am just so other people will think I'm easy going and nice. That is denying who I am, letting people step on me. I don't want to wake up one day and realize I didn't go all in, that I didn't take the risk of becoming the version of myself that I so badly want to be. One of the hardest and most terrifying things in life is following your passion. Realizing in my core that I want to be a writer, that I want to go out there and use my powers for others, that I want to embrace everything I am—with all my flaws—it's a burning desire inside me, and I am not going to let go of it ever again. My journey begins now, and for the first time in my life I am going to go to my father and confess all that I have been holding deep down inside. And if he rejects me, then that's the end of it. I will leave. After all, his house was never my home.

I drive to the penthouse in Zamalek. There are lots of guards downstairs. I don't know what is happening, but it seems like there is some kind of trouble. I park my car a short distance from the penthouse, so that no one can take it from me by force. Father deactivated all my Visa accounts, so I have nothing now except this car.

"Excuse me, where are you going?" A guard standing outside my father's building puts his hands on the door so I won't be able to pass.

"I live here," I tell him.

"I am sorry, but can you take off your sunglasses?" he asks. As I take them off, he steps closer, preventing me from entering. "I am sorry ma'am but you are not allowed up," he says. "I am going to politely ask you to leave please."

"What the hell are you talking about? I am Zayne Al-Ḥadidi's daughter. Let me pass," I shout.

"Yes, I know who you are and I have orders to not let you in," the guard says. "So once again, I am politely asking you to leave."

I feel my heart pounding and all the anger inside of me is turning into rage. I know that soon I will lose my mind. Luckily, as every woman knows, if a man hurts you, or in any way tries to get in your way, just kick him in the balls. I take a step back and look at the guard. I'm wearing my huge boots, and without any hesitation, I give him a massive kick that I know for sure he won't be getting up from anytime soon. He isn't expecting it, and instantly falls to the ground. I see more guards coming quickly towards me, so I run to the stairs. I am not going to climb all the way to the tenth floor using the stairs, so instead I stop on the fourth floor. I hear the guards running after me. I hide in a cupboard, the one we throw the trash in. It smells like dead cats in here. I wait for the footsteps to pass and I slowly go outside. I take the elevator to the tenth floor and find that none of the guards have got here yet.

I knock on the door, then ring the bell so many times, trying to give them a sign that it's me, that they should open the door quickly. "Open the door! These crazy people are not allowing me up! I don't know why! Open the door?" I scream, knocking hard on the door. Eventually, Fatma opens the door just a crack. She feels scared and sad and I wonder what has happened.

"Miss Malikah, I am very sorry but your father has banned you from this whole building," she says, crying. "I am sorry."

"What? What are you talking about, Fatma? Open the damn door." I try to push it but it's not opening any further.

Tina comes out from behind the door. "Hey, Malikah, long time no see. Sorry dear but your father is out. He has banned you from coming to the house. You ran away and he wants you to stay away. It's not like you were the daughter he wanted anyway," Tina says, pressing her hands to her stomach. It is bigger than when I last saw her. She is pregnant; they are having a baby together. I stare at her, trying to project all my anger and hate through just this one look. I run downstairs to see Noah. I knock on the door.

"Noah, open up. These people are crazy. They don't want me to come in," I scream and knock but no one opens the door. I start to cry. I'm panicking. But then Noah finally opens the door. He is all dressed up, probably going to work.

"Malikah," he says as he comes out of his house, closing the door behind him. He hands me a suitcase. "This is the rest of your clothes. Your father put them in trash bags, but I put them in this suitcase instead, so you wouldn't feel humiliated like your mother did. Sorry, I mean Dahliah," he hesitates. "You know what I mean." He is also feeling scared and sad.

"Why don't you let me in so that we can talk? I need to know what's going on," I ask.

"Malikah," he says gently. "I am afraid I can't let you in." He is staring at the ground. "Your father has given us all orders not to let you in our houses. The guards downstairs are all here to stop you coming anywhere near us."

I find that my knees are weak, and I am about to fall but I try to control myself. "Us? I thought that was you and me, not you and them." I break into a smile. "You are letting me go, banning me from your house like everyone else? Is that why Bilal left?"

"Bilal went away the day you left. I am assuming this was because he was in love with your mother. He wanted to keep an eye on you. Since you ran away, him and Zayne have been fighting almost nonstop, so I guess that's why," Noah says. "I am sorry, Malikah, I am just following orders but we can hang out somewhere else—I am still your cousin."

I laugh at his words, I can't believe what I am hearing, I can't believe what's happening. "Oh, because I would love to meet with you, sure. Afterall, you are my cousin," I say sarcastically. "What are you? I never knew that you could be such a coward. Go be a daddy's boy, Noah, you are not anything to me anymore."

"Malikah, please," Noah begs.

"Oh no, you please. Please don't call me or contact me in any way. I have no family now. You were the only family I had, but now I don't even have you. I hate you, just like I hate everyone behind that door upstairs. Of course, everyone is happy that the crazy person has left now."

"Your father thinks you are dangerous, since you set your clothes on fire. He thinks you need help."

"Yes, dear Father is always right. So tell me, Noah, is banning me his idea of help?" I ask sarcastically. "He won't help me by being a father, will he? He won't help me by letting me go to a therapist or anything. No, instead let's ban this crazy girl from the building!" I laugh.

"You are such a huge disappointment for me, Noah. I hope you soon realize it and when you do I hope it's not too late."

I hear the guards coming. They grab me, holding my hands behind my back and I scream, "Let me go, I will go on my own!"

"We don't trust you now," one of the guards says.

Noah watches the guards holding me back, sees them shouting in my face to shut up. They take me downstairs and throw me out of the building. I spit on the one who had been holding me back and go to my car. I sit in the car and cry. I can't believe my own father has banned me from ever going anywhere close to him again. But then I release that he must be in the office, since Noah was clearly dressed up for a meeting.

I drive to the office, crying all the way. Wearing my sunglasses and a cap, I enter the building. Everyone is too busy to notice me. I make my way to my father's office. I have to get this out of my system. I need confrontation, I need to confess, I need closure. I need relief from the pain I feel inside. I need to let out these words that are weighing me down.

I walk quickly, but act normally, like I am one of the employees here.

I reach my father's office and take a deep breath. Thank God his secretary isn't at her desk. Father usually prefers people to knock, but I just walk in anyway. I find his secretary on his lap, kissing his neck. He is holding her body, pressing it close to him. He finally sees me. I close the door, locking it behind me.

"Wow, the Father of the Year award goes to—" I say, laughing hysterically. "Man, there is a pregnant lady at your house. Are you going to ruin that baby's life too?"

His secretary stands up. Her boobs are hanging out. "Cover yourself, lady," I say to her. "That is so disgusting."

She runs to the door, but Father stops her. "Call the guards," he says. "Make her go away."

"I am not going anywhere until you hear what I have to say."

"I have no interest hearing anything from thieves and fuck ups like you."

"Thief? Maybe. Fuck up? I am not the one cheating on my pregnant wife here. You are going to listen or I will burn your whole fucking company down." Since he sees me as a threat, let's give him a real one. His secretary is still standing by the door.

"You are not going anywhere. Sit here." I push her towards a chair. She feels terrified. And he feels angry.

"You are not going anywhere until you hear me out."

"I am telling you I will not be listening. You are nothing to me now," he says and I try to let his words sink in. His emotions don't deny his words. So I know he doesn't love me anymore. I smile and try to find the words to say. He is not even looking at me; he is looking at his phone.

"I have a meeting in 10 minutes. That's all you've got," he says.

"Well," I pause. Confrontation is not easy for me, but anger is what is driving me now. "You have been the worst father anyone could have." *Good way to start out, lets force him to throw you out, get to the point, Malikah.* "You've lied to me all my life. You told me Mom couldn't come and visit, and I always asked why but you never had an answer. You lied to me about my whole existence. You banned my mothers from ever coming anywhere near me, just because you wanted me all for yourself. You just wanted to shape me into a version of you that would hold the company together and follow in your footsteps. But I am not like you, Dad."

It has been so long since I called him Dad. He finally looks up at me.

"I was trying to protect you, Malikah."

"Protect me? Who from? My mother? She died because of you," I scream.

"No. She died because she was mentally ill, she was a crazy woman."

"Mentally ill? Oh Father, we are all mentally ill in one way or another. You hurt her, manipulated her, physically abused her, and then forced her to sign papers to legally stop her from coming anywhere near me until I was twenty-one years old. Until I could make my own decisions."

"I cannot see you making any good decisions now," he says, laughing at me.

"Don't fucking laugh at me. Don't you dare! You are a cheater and a manipulator. You ruined my whole life and here I am! Look at me, Daddy! I am nothing like how you wanted me to be. I am not the person you planned I would be. I am nothing like you. In fact, I am way better than you, and I know this for sure. I don't hate or manipulate people; I don't go around imposing my powers and demanding others to be and do what I please. You are a self-centered narcissist and I hate you. I hate you for not letting me pursue my dreams. I hate you for trying to force me into a business marriage. I hate you for stopping my mother from coming anywhere near me, and then banning my real mother too. You forbid me from the one feeling that I needed the most. You took away my mother just because you wanted full control over who I am. But look at me now, huh?"

"Such a big disappointment if you ask me. Tell me, Malikah, are you a writer yet?" he asks, laughing again.

"I am going to be, and I am going to prove you wrong."

"Great, anything else?"

"I just wanted you to be my father, I wanted you to be true and to love me. I didn't ever need your money or your power. I just wanted you to be there. I wanted to feel like I had a home, but I never did. You made me realize so much by being the worst father anyone can be. But you know what? I forgive you anyway."

"I am not asking for your forgiveness! You are the one who should be asking for my forgiveness," he says angrily. "Tell me, is it better now that you know the real story?"

"Yes, it's way better, because I now know the truth. Now I know who I want to be. I am here to tell you that I am sorry, that's true. But I'm not sorry for going away, only for stealing your money and burning my clothes in the house. I am so glad I left, because without knowing what I know now I would have been depressed. I would probably have died with depression, because you forced me into everything. You wanted so badly to shape me, to turn me into that person that I am not. But I am my own person now, Dad, please just let it all go. We can be a family, a true one now."

Suddenly the secretary starts crying, she feels the intensity. I had forgotten she was there, and I ask her to leave. Now it's just me and him in the room, he doesn't have to act any more.

"We will never be a family. You are just like your disloyal, unworthy Uncle Bilal. You go out there trying so hard to be the person you are searching for, when I gave you a perfect place, somewhere that you belonged. You are an ungrateful shit," he screams.

"This is not who I am! Not everyone has to be like you. Some of us actually want to be something else. Some of us only find ourselves by letting this fucking family go. If only you had given me the freedom to be who I am, I wouldn't have left the house without asking. I knew you would stop me because, oh, anything other than what you planned for me to be is absolutely unacceptable. I wanted so badly to be my own self, to embrace who I am but you never let me. 'Wear that, be that, do that, obey me.' I am not your slave, I am your child. You should let me be my own person. You never let me, and it is even worse being a woman because going after what I want is probably unacceptable. But here I am, I ran away anyway, I found myself anyway, I now know my mother, and my biological mother. I got my closure, I found myself and here I am, Dad, talking to you in the most honest way, with no barriers, no hesitation, and no filters between us. Will you accept who I am now?"

He takes a deep breath and comes closer to me. His emotions are cold, and angry.

He then speaks in the simplest, calmest way possible.

"No, I will not accept who you are. If you are not built to be an Al-Hadidi, then you don't deserve to be a part of this family, and you certainly don't deserve to be my daughter. I should have left you the day you were born. You were such a huge disappointment. Women don't run away from their homes; it is disrespectful and unacceptable. This is just beyond anything that can be forgiven. You, my dear, are not forgiven."

I try to hold his hands before he leaves the room. I try to project my healing powers onto him, but he doesn't let me. He freaks out when I touch him and pushes me away as hard as he can. As I fall to the ground, he adjusts his clothes and looks down at me. "I don't like ungrateful people, you might think about that. You have no home here anymore, go be with your mommy. Oh, I thought you were my hope, but you turned out to be my pain and disappointment."

He closes the door behind him and leaves me there on the ground. I am crying as a security guard lifts me from the ground, takes me downstairs, and throws me out of the building. I see Father, Jabril, and Noah standing, watching. Then Karma runs towards me and hugs me tight for the very first time in our lives. She feels so much pain, so much anger.

"I am sorry about everything. I know we are not close but I wouldn't want anyone to go through this," she says. I hug her back and start crying.

Jabril screams for her to come. "Karma, come here immediately!"

Karma breaks the hug. "I know you will think that it's weird, me sympathizing with you. I know the whole story from Noah, and, Malikah, I can't wait for you to prove them all wrong." She smiles and lets me go.

I never knew Karma could be such a supportive, loving person. But I guess hard times show you who is truly going to be there, for real. I thought Noah would be there for me, but look at me, wrong again. Assuming another person to be true. Emotions can be changed and through this change you can understand so much about the person. Hard times help you to tell the real emotions from the fake ones. Someone can love you with all their hearts, like Noah loves me, but sometimes that's just not enough. Sometimes even people who love you don't understand what you are going through. And then there are people like Karma. Even though we are oil and water, she has never wanted to see me suffer. All she wanted was to be recognized, not ignored any more. I am no longer a threat to her, but this is not what she wanted either. She wanted us to be side by side. She was always jealous, but now I finally realize that it wasn't jealousy born of hate, she just wanted to fit in like everyone else. She has felt alone all this time, and I didn't listen. She felt like an outcast, just like me. She never had a real connection with anyone in the family, even her older brother was always closer to me. Sometimes the loneliest people are defensive and jealous, to avoid being sad.

I understand that now, because I can see that all Karma wanted was to belong. She had no idea that I didn't feel like I belonged either. People can go through the same exact thing, but feel and experience it in a completely different way. We are all different. Hard times have revealed Noah's true self. Embracing myself revealed that I can't be accepted by my own father. Learning to be myself has revealed that I've done the right thing, even if no one likes it at this point. Even though I am in pain and I feel lost, I know that I should have done this years ago. I go to my car and drive away; I can't stop crying. I can't stop replaying father's words to me, *You have no home, you are ungrateful, No I will not accept who you are*.

The whole day comes crashing down on my head, burning my heart and soul. I have no home, no money and nowhere to be. I think of Lina but I can't just ask for help from someone I barely know. I think of Bilal but I just don't want to pressure him with my problems anymore. I think of Sarah and although I really don't want to hurt her, she is the only one I can call now.

"Hello?" Sarah says, through my car speakers. She can hear me crying and she starts to panic. "Malikah, what's wrong? Talk to me!" But I can't talk. I feel like I've lost the ability to express myself. I feel like I can't find my words and I don't know what I can possibly say now.

"Okay baby, you don't have to talk. Can you come to me? I am at home. We can talk, okay? Just come here," Sarah says.

"Okay," I finally reply. "I will come to you."

"Send me a live location on WhatsApp? I want to know you are safe, please," Sarah says.

"Okay," I say, wiping my tears and trying to hold myself together. I send her my live location and drive in the direction of Sarah's house.

Chapter Thirty-Six

I have never been a fan of social media. I use it to get my poetry out there, and created the nickname I now use, "The Poet." Right now, I just want to tell people my story, to reveal my powers. To get out there with no fear. My whole family has already rejected me, how hard can other people's rejection be? I open Instagram and start a live video that I will save and post on IGTV later, for the whole world to see. I park my car at the side of the highway, set up my phone and start speaking my truth. There are only 4 people watching, but I don't care. I will talk anyway.

"Hello everyone, this is going to be a post for everyone to see," I start. "I have never done this before, and I only have five thousand followers, but I will talk anyway. And maybe my words will reach out to the ones who watch me, and maybe those people will actually feel what I am saying." I pause and take a deep breath. "This might sound crazy, but I have superpowers. I am a super empath. I can feel other people's emotions. I can help each and every one of you, if you let me. I can heal others too. I can calm the demons that have been eating you up. I know this sounds crazy, but it's true. I have done it many times, and you can ask the people closest to me—Sarah Zaki and Adam Ghazali. You can find them in my followers list."

I have no idea why I'm doing this, I just know that I have to let everyone know about my powers. I know I want to reach out for people and help people reach out for me. I want to discuss mental illness. I want to give people hope, even though that's the last thing I am feeling now. I guess a part of me opened this live stream to get myself out there, to say the words I have been trapping inside; to help myself as well as others, like a therapy session. An NF song, *Therapy Session* comes into my head. My powers are not just empathy but words too. I am a writer. I know how to express myself. Even though I had lost my words, I found them again when I realized I have to let myself go, get myself out there with no fear or shame about who I am.

"I am not ashamed of who I am; I know my whole family is disappointed but I am not. I followed what I believe is true and it's not easy to do that. It's also unacceptable for a middle eastern girl to follow anything when she knows that her family opposes her. But I don't care anymore because right now I know who I am. I am an empath; I have the power to heal others. I have the power to feel others and make them feel that they are not alone. I have the freedom to write whatever I want. And to pursue my dream of becoming a writer."

I still have to figure out where to go next, but all I can think about is Adam's smell and how safe I feel with him. He is the only one who sees through me and accepts who I am, even when I didn't accept myself. I can't yet get a grip on what I feel for Lina exactly, but I guess everything will fall into place as long as I follow the real me.

As I'm telling my story, more people start to watch. I talk about my mother's suicide and how the police asked me to cover it up. I talk about how my father forced my mothers to sign papers so he could ban them from seeing me. "He wanted to be the sole influence in my life, but look at me now, Dad! I'm breaking all your rules and becoming your biggest disappointment." I remember Linkin Park's song *Numb*. I used to listen to this song every day and imagine what it would be like to not follow my father's footsteps. I dreamed that maybe I could become my own person, rather than the person he wanted me to be. I spent my whole life trying to reach everyone's expectations; exceed them even. I tried to please everyone, and to be the best version of myself in their eyes. But as I was doing that, I lost hope and respect for myself. I lost what little self-confidence I had. I lost who I was, just to please others who didn't even care how depressed I became. My mother's death was the most tragic event in my life, and I know I will never be able to let it go. But at least I now understand that although some things don't go your own way, that doesn't mean they are going the wrong way. Without the heart-breaking tragedy of my mother's suicide, I wouldn't have found myself. I don't know if this was my mother's intention, but I know deep down that it's all part of God's plan.

I am not yet the whole person I want to be but I am one step closer every day. I can't deny my pain, but right now, I am expressing it in front of five thousand people. I will be loud. I don't know yet where I am going. I have no home. I don't know how many days I can keep my hopes up. I don't know if I can be anything at all. All I truly fear is going back. I never want to go back. I don't know if I can be with Adam at this stage in my life, or if I can ever accept Lina. I might have forgiven my father but I know deep down I will always hold the pain he made me feel. I'm not holding the pain out of hate, I am using it to motivate myself, to give myself strength.

I want to tell everyone my story, I want to give everyone the hope I lost waking up every day in my father's house.

"I honestly have no idea where to go," I say, smiling into my phone. These people must think I am crazy, but they keep sending me hearts and saying how they can't believe that I'm showing everyone my true reality on social media.

Part of me wants to be a writer because of my passion. But also another big part of me wants to be writer because of my pain. I want to reach out to people by using my words, using my passion to help others see the unseen. To feel the unfelt. To be the person they ought to be. Everything happens in time, but that doesn't mean that you have got to go out there and work your ass off to get it. Figuring out who you are, what you really want, is hard enough. Achieving it is even harder. But if I have learned one thing along this journey it would be that once you finally get there, you won't feel content. Instead you will feel whole. You will feel like a new person. Society, families and even friends around us force us to be something, and we force them too. Accepting that everyone should be their own person and follow their own free will fix so may problems in this world. I know that nothing is perfect. However, empathy and compassion is what we should follow. I am not saying we should sit and cry next to everyone feeling pain. Rather we should respect other people's emotions and the things they go through. This respect and acceptance are such profound feelings that will surely help humanity to rise from our current apathetic state.

"Life is not easy, but with a little more empathy and a little less ignorance this world will be beautiful. I am here to give you my powers, I am here to help you. I am here because I am just like all of you, lost in this land, trying to figure myself out. I am here to share this with everyone. I know now that this power shouldn't be mine alone. I know that this power is not a curse, but that instead I was sent here to be something. I was sent to help others. I was sent to heal and be healed. I have been hating myself and my powers all my life, and I don't need anyone to ask for help. I am offering everything that I am, so that I can hopefully make this world a little bit better. I am no superhero, and my powers may not seem cool. But I *am* a healer, a feeler, and a writer. This might be the first time I say this with my head held high.

"My name is Malikah, and I am a super empath. I am only here to help, to write, and to be myself. I think we should all do that. Thank you for listening."

Chapter Thirty-Seven

Part of life is tragedy and what is more tragic than death? Death is one way to warn you that you don't have all the time in the world. It also alerts you to the fact that sometimes experiencing death is the only way to realize who and where you belong.

I don't know if my emotional Instagram video will reach out to anyone. Or if anyone will even believe me, but I have never embraced my vulnerability before. I know it is wrong to post personal stuff on social media. But all I really intended was to let people know that my powers exist, and to let those who might have the same powers as me and Adam come out of the closet and show me who they are. It is not easy being an empath. It's not easy embracing vulnerability and the fragility of emotions. Humans run away from emotions because they believe emotions make them weak but no, emotions do not make you weak. Emotions are there to tell you something, you just need to listen carefully. Sometimes emotions are blurry, but they are still there and they are still real. I have lived my whole life believing that my powers make me weak, but I was wrong. My powers made me who I am and for that I am grateful.

I had a panic attack after I finished the video, and now I'm driving to Sarah's with red, puffy eyes. Suddenly a huge truck is coming straight at me, way too fast. The driver must be drunk. I feel the truck crash into the back of my car, and I hit my head on the steering wheel. My car spins around the highway and I feel it hit three more cars as it spins. My head smashes into the window next to me, the airbag finally comes out but the car is out of control and it turns over. I am upside down, sliding along the highway.

In this moment, I know that I will die. I know I am dying. I don't feel panic anymore. I just know that this is the end. I hope Sarah publishes my novel. I hope the world remembers me with my empathy. I hope everyone knows that I was only trying to help. I feel my soul detach from my body, and suddenly I am watching the whole accident from another person's perspective. I am standing right there, watching my body break and twist. I see the glass smash, and the whole car crumble.

My life isn't flashing before my eyes. No. All that I see are the things I didn't do; the things I didn't say. I see the things I should have done and the person I wished I'd become. All I see is how worthless my life has been. I see all the times I chose to please, the times I accepted manipulation. I see the time I have wasted by hating who I am, when I could have been something better, someone different. Someone brave. My life isn't flashing before my eyes, because I've had no life. All I had was orders and expectations. I see Adam and feel how he held me close. I see what could have been and everything we could have done together. I see Sarah, holding her Master's certificate. She is a valedictorian, a psychologist, and a perfect friend. I see my book how I hoped it would be. I see my mother's face, Dahliah's face, begging me to get up. She is screaming for me to get up, but I can't. I see Bilal, reaching out to my mother, trying to touch her. But he can't reach her. Oh, how I wish they had acted on their emotions. Maybe she wouldn't have been so miserable. Maybe she wouldn't have killed herself.

I am between life and death. Can I truly die peacefully? I wanted to do so much. I wanted to be so much. I wanted to help so much. But now that I am dying, there is no time to do, be, or say anything anymore. I try to close my eyes, to let my soul rest, but even my soul can't rest, knowing that I didn't fulfil my destiny. I didn't have the chance to be whole and complete. I didn't have the chance to embrace myself. I know I wanted to and I know I doubted myself so many times, but if I had one last chance, I would do it the right way.

I know I am dying; my life has ended and there is nothing I can do about it. But what if everyone just pursued what they wanted and what they believed in the first place? What if society, family, and traditions didn't stop you from being who you are? From embracing yourself, your potential and your dreams? What if we didn't let our doubts control us? What if we didn't let other people's opinions take over us? Because let me tell you something, when you are near death none of this matters. In the end it's not your life that's going to flash before your eyes. It's all the things you didn't do, the things you didn't go after, the things you didn't work for. The people you love will flash before your eyes, but you won't be able to reach them and they won't be able to reach you because you didn't embrace yourself, your potential, so they don't know who you are. They only know the version you were forced to be. Don't be forced. Life is short and hard. Follow your dream. Say what you feel. Be vulnerable and listen to your emotions. Be aware of them; they are trying to tell you something. Because when you are this close to death, these are the things that matter. Not society, not opinion, not traditions, not expectations. Not even your highest degree of education. Just you and your choices. Did you embrace who you are, with your empathy and compassion? Or were you the person you were forced to be? The person you grew up to believe you should be? This is not who you are. This is not who you are.

I am lying here on the ground, soaking with my own blood, finally dying. Finally reaching the peace of death. But I don't have peace. I just have loss, pain, and regrets. Don't do that to yourself. Nothing is ever worth losing who you are.

Chapter Thirty-Eight

I can't see. I feel like I am awake but I can't see. It is dark and I can't breathe. I keep twitching but I feel trapped. I feel a hand holding mine. It is a small hand, a woman's. Someone is trying to whisper something in my ear. I finally open up my eyes and I see a strong light. I don't see faces, I see blur, but the hand is still holding mine. Someone approaches me and removes a tube from my mouth and suddenly I can breathe again.

"Don't panic, I am here," someone says. The voice feels familiar but I can't see clearly yet. Someone, a man this time, picks up my other hand. The light is dimmed a little and I finally see clearly. I see Lina and Adam.

I try to speak, but my tongue feels so heavy. I can't move my body. I feel pain everywhere and I can't lift my head.

"You were in an accident," Lina says. "You've been in a coma for a week now. Just rest, my dear. All your senses will come back gradually. Just rest." I try to nod in agreement but I can't, so instead I motion with my eyes. Adam looks at me. His eyes are all puffy and red. I know immediately that he has been crying. I thought I was dying but I wasn't. I am still here. I don't know how to show excitement, but I try to smile and they smile back. Lina asks Adam to leave the room for a moment. She sits beside me on a chair, holding my hand in both of hers. I feel the warmth of her hands. I see the tears pouring down her face.

"I told you, Malikah, I will never leave you again." She takes a deep breath and says, "I was forced by your father to stay away from you, to not go anywhere near you. I wasn't in the picture and you never knew me but I want to tell you something." She leans in and kisses my hand. "My life truly started the day you stepped into my office. I knew you were angry; I knew you were scared but I didn't know that you were actually going to come to find me. I had planned a whole trip to come back to find you. But then you showed up, unannounced, claiming your right to know everything. I am so thankful for the courage that is inside of you. Although I don't think you have any idea how courageous and brave you really are." She stands up and leans in to kiss my forehead.

"But then again, you saved my life years ago, just by being a fetus inside me, growing. You changed me from a selfish person into who I am today, just by existing. You were taken away from me, and although that was so hard, and so unbearable to live with, it's what made me who I am today.

"I know it's hard for you to accept me, but I promise you I will be the mother I was supposed to be. It's not too late is it? Please give me this chance, Malikah, please." She starts crying and I caress her hand. I thought I was dying. I truly felt that it was the end. But waking up, listening to Lina saying all the things she needed to tell me, has made me realize how everything happens for a reason. Everything happens to lead you somewhere you never thought you would reach. I have a mother who loves me and despite all the bad things she has done in her life she admits and she regrets everything. But this is not what moves me. What truly moves me is that among all this pain, I wake up here and find her committing to her promise that she will always be there for me. She kisses my forehead again, then my cheek. And finally she says, "I love you, Malikah. I always did. Just give me a chance. I know you can't speak now but I will be waiting for your answer." She smiles.

Sarah comes into the room. "Oh, Malikah, thank God!" She rushes to my bed and kisses me. "I thought I was going to lose you! Don't do that to me, God damn it," she cries. I smile but a tear finds its way down my face. Adam follows Sarah and stands next to me, looking at me with tears in his eyes. I know he can't begin to express his feelings. I know that if I was about to lose him I would probably lose my mind. So I smile at him and he smiles back then leans down toward me. "I love you so much," he whispers. "You are so beautiful, you know that?"

I smile. "I love you," I finally say in a heavy, low voice.

"I thought I lost you," he says, kneeling on the ground, holding my hand, and kissing it. "Thank God I can breathe again."

Bilal knocks, even though the door is open. He will never be like the other Hadidi men. He enters the room holding what seems like a canvas, but it's covered up and I can't see what it is. He looks at me, smiling, and I manage to smile back. He turns his happy face to Lina and she smiles too.

Looking at me, Lina says, "Bilal has been here the whole time you've been in a coma. He's been going home each night and coming back each morning." She looks up at him and asks, "Is it ready?"

"Yes" he replies, nodding, and tears the cover off the canvas. I see it. It is a beautiful painting full of color and darkness. There is a woman standing in the middle of the picture. She has a blurry face, but I can see that she is holding her heart. She is surrounded by darkness but she is bright, like lightning in the night. Bilal takes a deep breath and looks at me.

"This is you," he tells me gently. "I painted it myself. It is probably my best painting yet." He smiles. "You are fighting the darkness with your heart. You are lighting the world with your powers. I have always known you were different, I never grasped how different you were, but I always felt in my heart that you were special, I just knew it. The only woman I painted before this was your beautiful mother, Dahliah. So it felt right that I should also paint you."

He leans in and kisses my forehead, too carefully, like he is scared of hurting me. "Malikah, you are the hero in so many stories, but you don't even know it. This painting is my gift for you. It is my way of saying thank you for giving me hope and for picking me up even when you needed to be picked up yourself. Thank you."

He smiles and it's the most beautiful smile I have ever seen.

Noah and Karma come into my room. They are holding flowers and chocolates. Noah looks down, avoiding eye contact, but I know that he means well. Even though we will never be the same with each other, I knew he would come.

Karma comes over to me. "You made quite a buzz on social media, now everyone wants to know you and follow you!" she smiles. "I guess that was the plan."

I smile and say, "No, just helping."

"Well, you need to get better quickly, because you had an email yesterday. An agent wants to meet you in person and talk about your book!" Sarah tells me. "I couldn't wait to tell you!"

I start tearing up and she hugs me, then Adam hugs me, then Lina hugs me, and for the first time in so long I feel like I belong. I feel like I have a home. I feel like I am actually so much closer to achieving everything I have dreamed of. I will be a writer. I will embrace my powers and use it to help others.

I will be myself, because that is the best thing anyone can be.